DEATH of a
DUSTMAN

The Hamish Macbeth series

DEATH of a DUSTMAN

A Hamish Macbeth Murder Mystery

M. C. BEATON

ROBINSON
London

Constable & Robinson Ltd
3 The Lanchesters
162 Fulham Palace Road
London W6 9ER
www.constablerobinson.com

First published in the USA by Grand Central Publishing,
a division of Hachette Book Group USA, Inc.

This edition published by Robinson,
an imprint of Constable & Robinson, 2009

A copy of the British Library Cataloguing in
Publication data is available from the British Library

UK ISBN: 978-1-84901-078-8

Printed and bound in the EU

1 3 5 7 9 10 8 6 4 2

For Olivia and Gwenda Peters
with much love

Hamish Macbeth fans share their reviews . . .

'Treat yourself to an adventure in the Highlands; remember your coffee and scones – for you'll want to stay a while!'

'I do believe I am in love with Hamish.'

'M. C. Beaton's stories are absolutely excellent . . . Hamish is a pure delight!'

'A highly entertaining read that will have me hunting out the others in the series.'

'A new Hamish Macbeth novel is always a treat.'

'Once I read the first mystery I was hooked . . . I love her characters.'

Share your own reviews and comments at
www.constablerobinson.com

Chapter One

Love in a hut, with water and a crust,
Is – Love, forgive us! – cinders, ashes, dust.
                                        – John Keats

They are still called dustmen in Britain. Not rubbish collectors or sanitation engineers. Just dustmen, as they were called in the days of George Bernard Shaw's *Pygmalion* and Charles Dickens's *Our Mutual Friend*.

Lochdubh's dustman, Fergus Macleod, lived in a small run-down cottage at the back of the village with his wife, Martha, and four children. He was a sour little man, given to drunken binges, but as he timed his binges to fall between collection days, nobody paid him much attention. It was rumoured he had once been an accountant before he took to the drink. No one in the quiet Highland village in the county of Sutherland at the very north of Scotland could ever have imagined he was a sleeping monster, and one that was shortly about to wake up.

* * *

Mrs Freda Fleming had recently bullied her way on to Strathbane Council to become Officer for the Environment. This had been a position created for her to shut her up and keep her out of other council business. She was the only woman on the council. Her position in the chauvinist Highlands was due to the fact that the ambitious widow had seduced the provost – the Scottish equivalent of mayor – after a Burns Supper during which the normally rabbity little provost, Mr Jamie Ferguson, had drunk too much whisky.

Mrs Fleming nursed a private dream and that was to see herself on television. Her mirror showed a reflection of a well-upholstered woman of middle years with gold-tinted hair and a pugnacious face. Mrs Fleming saw in her glass someone several inches slimmer and with dazzling charisma. Her husband had died three years previously. He had been a prominent businessman in the community, running an electronics factory in Strathbane. His death from a heart attack had left Mrs Fleming a very wealthy widow, with burning ambition and time on her hands. At first she had accepted the post of Officer for the Environment with bad grace but had recently woken to the fact that Green was in – definitely in.

She figured if she could think up some grand scheme to improve the environment, the cameras would roll. She firmly believed she was born to be a television star. Strathbane was much in need of improvement. It was a blot on the Highlands, a sprawling town full of high rises, crime, unemployment and general filth. But it was too huge a task and not at all photogenic. She aimed for national television, and national television would go for something photogenic and typically Highland. Then she remembered Lochdubh, which she had visited once on a sunny day. She would 'green' Lochdubh.

One hot summer's morning, she arrived in Lochdubh. The first thing she saw was smelly bags of rubbish lined up outside the church hall. This would not do. She swung round and glared along the waterfront. Her eye fell on the blue lamp of a police station, partly obscured by the rambling roses which tumbled over the station door.

She strode towards it and looked over the hedge. Hamish Macbeth, recently promoted to police sergeant, was playing in the garden with his dog, Lugs.

'Ahem!' said Mrs Fleming severely. 'Where is the constable?'

Hamish was not in uniform. He was wearing an old checked shirt and baggy cords. The sun shone down on his flaming red hair and pleasant face.

3

He smiled at her. 'I am Sergeant Macbeth. Can I help you?'

'What has happened to Lochdubb?' she demanded.

'Lochdubh,' corrected Hamish gently. 'It's pronounced Lochdoo.'

'Whatever.' Mrs Fleming did not like to be corrected. 'Why is all that smelly rubbish outside the church hall?'

'We had a fête to raise money for charity,' said Hamish. 'Who are you?'

'I am Mrs Freda Fleming, Officer for the Environment in Strathbane.'

'Well, Mrs Fleming, like I was saying, it's because of the fête, all that rubbish.'

'So why hasn't it been collected?'

'Fergus Macleod, that's the dustman, doesn't collect anything outside collection day. That's not for a couple of days' time.'

'We'll see about that. Where does he live?'

'If you go to Patel's, the general store, and go up the lane at the side, you'll find four cottages along the road at the back. It's the last one.'

'And why aren't you in uniform?'

'Day off,' said Hamish, hoping she wouldn't check up.

'Very well. You will be seeing more of me. I plan to green Lochdubh.' With that, she strode off along the waterfront, leaving Hamish scratching his fiery hair in bewilderment. What on earth could she have meant? Perhaps trees or maybe gardens?

But he had enough problems to fill his brain without worrying about Mrs Fleming's plans. Behind him and, he hoped, manning the police office was his new constable, Clarry Graham. Clarry was a lazy slob. He had never progressed from the ranks. He rarely washed and slopped around in a shiny old uniform.

Then there was the problem of the new hotel. The Lochdubh Hotel at the harbour had stood vacant for some years. It had recently been bought by a Greek entrepreneur, George Ionides. This meant work for the villagers and Hamish was glad of that, but on the other hand he was aware that a new hotel would take custom away from the Tommel Castle Hotel, run by Colonel Halburton-Smythe, whose glamorous daughter, Priscilla, had once been the love of his life.

He went into the police station followed by Lugs. *Lugs* is the Scottish for 'ears', and he had called the dog that because of its large ears. In the police station, the fat figure of Clarry was snoring gently behind the desk.

I should wake him up, thought Hamish, but what for? It's as quiet as the grave these days. Clarry had strands of grey hair plastered across his pink scalp and a large grey moustache which rose and fell with every somnolent breath. He had a round pink face, like that of a prematurely aged baby. His chubby hands were folded across his stomach. The only thing in his favour was that he was a good cook and no one could call him mean. Most of his salary went on food – food which he was delighted to cook for Hamish as well as himself.

Oh, well, thought Hamish, closing the office door gently. I could have got someone worse.

Fergus was in the middle of one of his binges, and had he been at home Mrs Fleming would have seen to it that he lost his job. But Fergus was lying up in the heather on the moors, sleeping off his latest binge, so it was his wife, Martha, who answered the door. Martha had once been a pretty girl, but marriage, four children and multiple beatings had left her looking tired and faded. Her once thick black hair was streaked with grey and her eyes held a haunted look.

Mrs Fleming questioned her closely about her husband and fear prompted Martha to protect the horrible Fergus, for what would they live on if he lost his job? She said he was a hard worker, and the reason he collected the rubbish only once a week was because he had one of those old-fashioned trucks where everything had to be manually lifted into it by hand. Mrs Fleming was pleased by Martha's timid, deferential air. She gave Martha her card and said that Fergus was to report to the council offices at eleven the following morning. 'We must see about getting him a new truck,' she said graciously. 'I have plans for Lochdubh.'

After she had gone, Martha told her eldest, Johnny, to take care of the younger ones, and she then set out to look for her husband. By evening, she had almost given up and was leaning wearily over the hump-backed bridge over the River Anstey.

She found herself hoping that he was dead. That would be different from him losing his job. She could get her widow's pension, and when the third child, Sean, was of school age, she could maybe work a shift at the new hotel if she could get someone to look after the baby. Mrs Wellington, the minister's wife, had challenged her with the unsympathetic, 'You must have known he was a drunk when you married him,' but she had not. Certainly he seemed to like his dram like a lot of Highlanders. She had met him at a wedding in Inverness. He had said he was an accountant and working over at Dingwall. He had courted her assiduously. It was only after they were married and he had moved into the cottage she had inherited from her parents that it transpired he had no job and was a chronic drunk. It also transpired he really had been an accountant, but he had seemed to take a savage delight in becoming the village dustman. Then she sensed, rather than saw, his approach.

She swung round, her back to the parapet of the bridge. He came shambling towards her with that half-apologetic leer on his face

7

that he always had when he had sobered up between binges.

'Looking for me?'

'Aye, a woman from the council in Strathbane called. Wants to see you in Strathbane on the morrow.'

'Whit about?'

'Didnae say. She left her card.'

'You should've asked.' Fergus had become wizened with drink, although only in his mid-forties. He had a large nose and watery eyes and a small prissy mouth. He had rounded shoulders and long arms, as if all the lifting of dustbins had elongated them. It was hard for Martha to think that she had loved him once.

'I'd better go and see her,' grumbled Fergus.

Martha shivered although the evening was balmy and warm. She had a feeling the bad times were coming. Then she chided herself for her fancies. How could the bad times come when they were already here?

Clarry slid a plate of steaming bouillabaisse in front of Hamish Macbeth. 'Try that, sir,' he ordered. 'Nobody can make the bouillabaisse like Clarry.'

'Aye, you're a grand cook, Clarry,' said Hamish, thinking he would settle for fish fingers and frozen chips if only Clarry would turn out to be a good policeman instead.

But the fish stew was delicious. 'Did you

ever think of going into the restaurant business?' asked Hamish. 'A genius like you shouldnae be wasting your talents in the police force. The Tommel Castle Hotel could do with a good chef.'

'It's not the same,' said Clarry. 'You go to them grand hotels and they would want ye to cut corners, skimp on the ingredients to save money.' He ate happily.

'There was a woman here from the council in Strathbane. Wanted to see Fergus.'

'The drunk?'

'Himself. Maybe you could do something for me, Clarry. I've tried, God knows. I'm pretty sure he beats that wife o' his. Go along there tomorrow and see if you can get her on her own, and tell her she doesn't need to put up with it.'

'Domestics were never my scene,' said Clarry, tearing off a hunk of bread and wiping the last of the soup from the bottom of his plate.

'You're a policeman,' said Hamish sharply. 'We don't leave wives to be battered by their husbands any more.'

'I'll give it a try,' said Clarry amiably. 'Now when you've finished that, I've got a nice apple pie hot in the oven.'

Fergus drove over to Strathbane the following morning in the refuse truck. He was dressed in

9

his only suit, a dark blue one, carefully brushed and cleaned by his wife. His sparse hair was brushed and oiled over his freckled pate.

He could feel anger rising up in him against the villagers of Lochdubh. One of them must have reported him for something. He would try to find out who it was and get even.

And so he drove on, one sour little cell of blackness hurtling through the glory of the summer Highlands, where the buzzards soared free above and the mountains and moors lay gentle in the mellow sun.

In Strathbane, he parked outside the square, concrete Stalinist block that was Strathbane Council offices. He gave his name at the reception desk and asked for Mrs Fleming.

A secretary arrived to lead him up the stairs to the first floor. Mrs Fleming had commandeered one of the best offices. Fergus was ushered in. His heart sank when he saw Mrs Fleming. Like most bullies, he was intimidated by other bullies, and in Mrs Fleming's stance and hard eyes and by the very way those eyes were assessing him, he recognized a bully.

'Sit down, Mr Macleod,' said Mrs Fleming. 'We are to discuss the greening of Lochdubh.'

Fergus's now sober brain worked rapidly. This woman was one of those Greens. Very well. He would play up to her.

'I'm aye keen of doing anything I can to protect the environment, Mrs Fleming.'

'Splendid. Why then, however, did you not collect the rubbish piled up outside the church hall?'

'If you take a look down from your window, missus, you'll see my truck. It's one o' thae old ones with the sliding doors at the side.'

Mrs Fleming walked to the window, and he joined her. 'Now, I hae to lift all the rubbish into that myself. No help. I'm getting treatment for my back. I can manage fine if I keep to the collection day, which is Wednesday.'

Mrs Fleming scowled down at the old truck. Not photogenic.

She strode back to her desk. 'Sit down, Mr Macleod. That truck will not do. I plan to make an example of Lochdubh.' From beside her desk she lifted up a black plastic box. 'Boxes like these will be given to each householder. Waste paper, bottles and cans will be put into these boxes and not in with the general rubbish. Wheelie bins will be supplied.'

Fergus thought of those huge plastic bins on wheels. 'I couldnae lift those,' he protested.

'You won't need to,' said Mrs Fleming triumphantly. 'Your new crusher truck will have a mechanism for lifting the bins in. We will also put large containers on the waterfront at Lochdubh. One will be for wastepaper, the other for cans and the third for bottles.'

'But if they've tae put the cans and bottles and stuff in the black boxes, why will they need the extra bins?'

'So that they have no excuses for not separating their rubbish if they've got extra stuff. The hotels and boarding houses will need to use the larger bins.' She leaned forward. 'We are going to put Lochdubh on the map, Mr Macleod. How much do you earn?'

Fergus told her. 'We will double that. You are now promoted to Lochdubh's own environment officer. What do you wear while working?'

'Overalls and old clothes,' said Fergus.

'No, that won't do for the television cameras.'

'Television cameras?' echoed Fergus.

'Yes, when you have succeeded in making Lochdubh a model village, I will come with the provost and various dignitaries. Press and television will be there. You must have an appropriate uniform.' She looked at her watch. 'Now, if you will be so good, I would like you to wait here. I have a meeting with the other members of the council.'

Clarry, with his broad pink face sweating under his peaked cap, ambled up to Fergus's cottage. He knew Fergus had four children because Hamish had told him, and because it was the school holidays, he expected to see them playing around. There was a baby in a battered pram outside the door. He waggled his fingers at the baby, who stared solemnly back. Clarry knocked at the door.

Martha answered it and stepped back with a little cry of alarm when she saw his uniform. 'Just a friendly call,' said Clarry. 'Mind if I come in?'

'I'm just getting the children their lunch.'

The children – Johnny, ten years old, Callum, eight and Sean, four – were sitting round a table. They looked at him as solemnly as the baby had done.

'What are they having for lunch?' asked Clarry, his mind always on food.

'Baked beans on toast.'

Martha looked so tired and white and the children so unnaturally quiet that Clarry's heart was touched. 'You all need feeding up,' he said. 'You just wait here. I'll do the lunch for you.'

'But that's not necessary . . .' began Martha, but with a cheery wave, Clarry was moving off with the lightness and speed which makes some fat men good dancers.

He returned after half an hour carrying two heavy shopping bags. 'Now if you'll just show me the kitchen.'

Martha led him into a small narrow kitchen. 'Off you go and watch telly,' said Clarry. 'Food on the table in a minute.'

Martha switched on the television and the children joined her on the sofa. Clarry beat sirloin steaks paper thin and tossed them in oil and garlic. He heated garlic bread in the oven.

13

He tossed salad in a bowl. He chopped potatoes and fried a mountain of chips.

Soon they were all gathered around the table. 'There's Coca-Cola for you lot,' said Clarry, beaming at the children, 'and Mum and I will have a glass o' wine.'

The children gazed at this large, expansive, friendly man. Johnny thought he looked like Santa Claus. They ate busily.

'I'm afraid we're costing you a lot of money,' said Martha.

'I put it on my boss's account,' said Clarry.

Under the influence of the wine and good food, Martha showed ghostlike signs of her earlier prettiness. But all the time, she was dreading her husband's return. Clarry talked about his days of policing in Strathbane while the children listened and Martha began to relax. Her husband could hardly make a scene with a policeman in the house.

After lunch, the children settled down in front of the television set again. 'No, no, that won't be doing at all on such a fine day,' said Clarry. 'Mum and I'll do the dishes and then it's outside with the lot of you.'

'Why did you come?' asked Martha, as Clarry washed and she dried.

'Just to say that if your man is beating you, you should report it,' said Clarry.

'He's not beating me,' said Martha. 'Besides, say he was, I couldn't support the children. They'd be taken away from me.'

Clarry looked down at her fragile figure. 'That would not happen for I would not let it happen, lassie. That's the lot. Now let's see if we can give those kids of yours some exercise.'

Clarry improvised a game of rounders with a broom handle and an old tennis ball. The children ran about screaming with laughter. Martha felt tears welling up in her eyes. When had she last heard her children laugh?

'So that's settled then,' said Mrs Fleming triumphantly as the members of the council looked back at her, feeling as if they had all been beaten and mugged. In vain had they protested at the cost of the proposed scheme. Mrs Fleming had bulldozed her way through all their objections.

She returned to her office where Fergus was waiting patiently. She took a tape measure out of her drawer. 'Now I'll just measure you for that uniform.'

Fergus felt bewildered. He had double the salary, and not only that, he had a chance to bully the villagers. Not one can or bottle or newspaper should make their appearance in the general rubbish. He began to feel elated. The good times were coming. The thought of a drink to celebrate flickered through his brain, but he dismissed it. As Mrs Fleming measured and made notes, he felt increasingly buoyed up by his new status.

He, Fergus Macleod, was now an environment officer.

Martha, from the position of her cottage, could see part of the winding road that led into Lochdubh. She also knew the sound of the rubbish truck's engine.

'Dad's coming!' she shouted.

Clarry thought that it was as if the game of rounders had turned into a game of statues. The children froze in mid-action. The sound of the truck roared nearer. Then they crept into the house. 'You'd better go,' said Martha to Clarry.

'Remember, lassie,' said Clarry, 'I'm just down the road. You don't need to put up with it.'

She nodded, her eyes wide and frightened, willing him to go.

Clarry ambled off and turned the corner to the waterfront just as Fergus's truck roared past.

Fergus parked the truck. Martha went out to meet him. Her husband's first words made her heart sink. 'We're going to celebrate tonight.'

Celebration usually only meant one thing. But Fergus was more eager for his new job than for any drink. He carried a box of groceries into the kitchen. There was Coke and crisps and chocolates for the children. There was an odd assortment of groceries – venison pâté, various exotic cheeses, parma ham, bottled cherries and cans of fruit. Martha thought wistfully of Clarry's offering of steak.

'What are we celebrating?' she asked timidly.

'I am Lochdubh's new environment officer,' said Fergus. He proudly told her of his increased salary, of the new truck, of the greening of Lochdubh.

For the Macleod family, it was a strangely relaxed evening. Martha prayed that the children would not mention Clarry's visit, and, to her relief, they did not. They had become so wary of their father's rages that they had learned to keep quiet on all subjects at all times.

For the next few weeks it seemed as if success was a balm to Fergus's normally angry soul. He even chatted to people in the village. Clarry felt obscurely disappointed. He had been nourishing private dreams of being a sort of knight errant who would rescue Martha from a disastrous marriage.

Martha had never known Fergus to go so long without a drink before. She was still frightened of him, like someone living perpetually in the shadow of an active volcano, but was grateful for the respite.

Then one morning, flyers were delivered to each household in Lochdubh announcing a meeting to be held in the church hall to discuss improvements to Lochdubh.

Hamish, along with nearly everyone else, went along.

Mrs Fleming was on the platform. She was wearing a black evening jacket, glittering with black sequins, over a white silk blouse. Her long black skirt was slit up one side to reveal one stocky, muscular leg in a support stocking. She announced the Great Greening of Lochdubh. Villagers listened, bewildered, as they learned that they would need to start separating the rubbish into various containers. New bottle banks and paper banks would be placed on the waterfront on the following day.

'What's a bottle bank?' whispered Archie Maclean, a fisherman.

'It's one o' thae big bell-shaped metal bins, like they have outside some of the supermarkets in Strathbane. You put your bottles in there.'

'Oh, is that what they're for,' said Archie. 'Oh, michty me! Waud you look at that!'

Mrs Fleming had brought Fergus on to the platform. The other members of the council had suggested that a uniform of green overalls would be enough, but Mrs Fleming had given the job of designing the uniform to her nephew, Peter, a willowy young man with ambitions to be a dress designer.

The audience stared in amazement as Fergus walked proudly on to the platform. His uniform was pseudo-military, bright green and with epaulettes and brass buttons. On his head he wore a peaked cap so high on the crown and so shiny on the peak that a Russian officer would kill for it. He looked for all the world like the wizened dictator of some totalitarian regime.

Someone giggled, then someone laughed out loud, and then the whole hall was in an uproar. Fergus stood there, his long arms hanging at his sides, his face red, as the gales of laughter beat upon his ears. He hated them. He hated them all.

He would get even.

The following day Hamish strolled down to the harbour to watch the work on the new hotel. Jobs were scarce in the Highlands, and he was pleased to see so many of the locals at work.

'Hamish?'

He swung round. Priscilla Halburton-Smythe stood there. He felt for a moment that old tug at his heart as he watched the clear oval of her face and the shining bell of her hair. But then he said mildly, 'Come to watch the rivals at work, Priscilla?'

'Something like that. It worries me, Hamish. We've been doing so well. They're going to take custom away from us.'

'They haven't any fishing rights,' said Hamish easily. 'That's what most of your guests come for – the fishing. And you don't take coach parties.'

'Not yet. We may have to change our ways to compete.'

'I haven't seen a sign of the new owner yet,' remarked Hamish.

'I believe he's got hotels all over Europe.'

'Any of your staff showing signs of deserting?'

'Not yet. But oh, Hamish, what if he offers much higher wages? We'll really be in trouble.'

'Let's see what happens,' said Hamish lazily. 'I find if you sit tight and don't do anything, things have a way of resolving themselves.'

'How's your new constable getting on?'

Hamish sighed. 'I thought the last one, Willie Lamont, was a pain with his constant cleaning and scrubbing and not paying any attention to his work. One new cleaner for sale and he was off and running. Now I've got Clarry. That's the trouble wi' living in Lochdubh, Priscilla. At Strathbane, they say to themselves, now which one can we really do without, and so I get Clarry. Oh, he's good-natured enough. And he's a grand cook, but he smells a bit and he iss damn lazy.' Hamish's accent always became more sibilant when he was upset. 'If he doesn't take a bath soon, I'm going to tip him into the loch.'

Priscilla laughed. 'That bad?'

'That bad.'

'And what's all this greening business?'

'It's that bossy woman. You weren't at the church hall?'

'No.'

'She is from the council, and she wants us to put all our rubbish into separate containers. There come the big bins.'

Priscilla looked along the waterfront. A crane was lifting the first of the huge bell-shaped objects into place. 'We don't like change,' she said. 'They'll rebel. They won't put a single bottle or newspaper in any of those bins.'

'Ah, but you haven't seen the green dustman yet. There he is!'

Fergus, resplendent in his new uniform, had appeared. He was standing with his hands behind his back, rocking on his heels, his face shadowed by his huge peaked cap.

'Heavens,' said Priscilla faintly. 'All he needs to complete that ensemble is a riding crop or a swagger stick.'

'I think that uniform means trouble,' said Hamish. 'Have you noticed that traffic wardens and people like that turn into fascist beasts the moment they get a uniform on?'

'A dustman can't do much.'

'He can do a lot in the way of petty bullying. The Currie sisters didn't give Fergus a Christmas box, and he didn't collect their rubbish until they complained to the council.'

21

'Well, there you are. Any bullying, they'll all complain to the council, and then it'll stop.'

'If that Fleming woman will listen to anyone.'

'What's her game? Is she a dedicated environmentalist? It said on the flyer that she was in charge of the council's environment department.'

'I think, talking of bullies, that she likes to find ways of spending the taxpayers' money to order people around. In fact, here she comes.'

Mrs Fleming drove along the waterfront while they watched. She got out of the car. Fergus strutted up to her.

Priscilla exploded into giggles. 'Would you believe it, Hamish? Fergus *saluted* her.'

Hamish laughed as well. The summer days and lack of crime on his beat were making him lazier than ever and dulling his usual intuition. He did not guess that Fergus's silly salute would make Mrs Fleming not hear one word against him, and so set in train a chain of events which would lead to horror.

Chapter Two

The wretch, concentred all in self,
Living, shall forfeit fair renown,
And, doubly dying, shall go down
To the vile dust from whence he sprung.
Unwep't, unhonor'd, and unsung.

                 – Sir Walter Scott

The next collection day passed without incident, and the following one. But then the boxes and wheelie bins were delivered and Fergus began to take his revenge.

The elderly Currie sisters, Nessie and Jessie, were the first victims. This was very unfair for they were among the few residents who had actually separated their rubbish into boxes and had put the rest into the wheelie bin. They found the boxes had been emptied of cans, bottles and papers, but the wheelie bin was still full and on it was a note on green paper.

It said, 'Garden rubbish is to be burnt. F. Macleod. Environment Officer.'

'What does he mean, "garden rubbish"?' asked Nessie. 'We haven't got any.'

'Haven't got any,' echoed her sister, who had the irritating habit of repeating the last words anyone, including herself, said. 'I'll get a chair, get a chair.' For the bin was too large for the small sisters to look into easily.

Jessie carried out a kitchen chair and, standing on it, lifted the plastic lid and peered down into the bin. 'There's just those dead roses, the ones that were in the vase, that we threw out, threw out.'

'I'm going to write to the council,' said Nessie.

'He hasn't taken the rubbish,' complained Clarry.

'Where's the wee man's wretched wheelie bin?' asked Hamish. 'You're supposed to use it, not leave it in bags.'

'Och, I thought that wheelie bin would be grand for the hen feed,' said Clarry.

Hamish sighed. 'Get it out and put the rubbish into it, Clarry. We're now living under a dictatorship.'

And so it happened all round the village. After all, it was the villagers some years ago who had taken away the network-type metal baskets from the waterfront to use as lobster pots.

24

Highland ingenuity had therefore found many uses for the wheelie bins other than the one for which they were intended. They were used to store all sorts of implements and cattle feed. Children played games at wheeling each other up and down the waterfront in them and their parents duly received threatening green notes from the dustman.

Letters of complaint poured into Strathbane Council. Mrs Fleming hailed originally from Hamilton in Lanarkshire. She thought all Highlanders were lazy and difficult and just plain weird. And so she did not trouble to answer even one of the letters. She told her secretary to throw them all away.

'I've got a wee job for you, Clarry,' said Hamish. 'Our job is to protect everyone in this village and that includes a pest like Fergus Macleod. Get round there and tell him to go easy. He's leaving rubbish uncollected for this reason and that reason, and the atmosphere is getting ugly.'

Clarry brightened at the thought of seeing Martha again. 'Right, sir.'

'And Clarry. Order yourself a new uniform from Strathbane.'

Clarry looked down at his round figure. 'Why?'

'That one's all old and shiny, and when did you last have a bath?'

Clarry blushed and hung his head.

'Aye, well, why don't you nip into the bathroom and have a bath, and I'll do what I can wi' your uniform.'

Clarry meekly went off to the bathroom. Hamish opened up the ironing table in the kitchen and began to sponge and clean and press Clarry's uniform.

In the bathroom, Clarry wallowed in the hot water like a whale. Then he towelled himself dry and opened the bathroom cupboard and peered at the contents. There was an unopened bottle of Brut on the top shelf. Clarry lifted it down and opened it, and then splashed himself liberally with it. He put on clean underwear and shambled into the kitchen and collected his cleaned and pressed uniform from Hamish with a muttered, 'Thanks.'

Hamish reeled back a bit before what smelled like a tidal wave of Brut, but charitably said nothing, hoping that the fresh air would mitigate the smell once Clarry was on his way.

Clarry walked slowly along the waterfront. It was another beautiful day. Recipes ran through his mind. He stopped outside the Italian restaurant and studied the menu.

'Anything you fancy, Officer?'

Clarry turned round and found himself facing an elderly man. 'I'm Ferrari, the owner,' the man said.

'I like Italian food,' said Clarry amiably, 'but I hope you don't use too much basil. That's the trouble these days. People go mad wi' the herbs and everything smells great and tastes like medicine.'

'You like cooking?'

'It's my hobby,' said Clarry proudly.

Mr Ferrari eyed him speculatively. Hamish's previous constable, the cleanliness freak, Willie Lamont, had left the police force to marry Ferrari's pretty relative Lucia. The restaurant chef was leaving at the end of the month.

'You must come for a meal one evening,' said Mr Ferrari. 'As my guest, of course.'

'That's very kind of you, sir,' said Clarry. He had a sudden dream of sitting in the restaurant in the evening, looking at Martha in the candlelight. Her husband couldn't stay sober that long, he might even drop dead, and then . . . and then . . . He beamed at Mr Ferrari. 'I might take you up on that offer. Would it be all right if I brought a lady?'

'My pleasure, Officer. Now you can do something for me. That dustman is picking through the restaurant rubbish and leaving most of it. We have too many cans and bottles to put into those little boxes.'

'I'm on my way to have a word with him.'

'Good. Between ourselves, Officer, it is time you did. The feeling against that man is running high, and if he is not stopped, something nasty might happen to him.'

27

I wish it would, thought Clarry as he touched his cap and walked away.

Clarry had never married. He had entered the police force because his mother had thought it a good idea. He had lived with his mother until her death a year before his move to Lochdubh. Lazy and unambitious, he had never risen up the ranks. His mother had seen off any woman who looked interested in him. The policewomen he had occasionally worked with terrified him. He privately thought the move to Lochdubh was the best thing that had ever happened to him. He loved the village. He liked his kind, laid-back boss. He thought again of Martha. There was something about her faded prettiness, her crushed appearance, that touched his heart. He turned up the lane leading to Martha's cottage. In his heart, he hoped against hope that the dustman would not be at home.

The baby was in its pram outside. Clarry made clucking noises at it and then rapped on the door. The eldest boy, Johnny, opened the door. 'Father at home?' asked Clarry.

The boy looked nervously over his shoulder. Fergus appeared. He was wearing an old shirt and jeans. 'What is it?' he snapped.

'May I come in?' asked Clarry.

'No, we'll talk outside.'

Fergus walked out and shut the door behind him.

Clarry removed his peaked cap and tucked

it under one arm. 'It's like this, sir. You are causing a great deal of distress among the villagers. You are not collecting their rubbish, and you are leaving nasty wee notes.'

'And what's that to you? It's a council matter. Any complaints and they can write to the council.'

'I am here to warn you, you might be in danger.'

Fergus snickered. 'From this bunch o' wimps? Forget it.'

Over the dustman's shoulder, Clarry could see Martha at the window. She gave him a wan smile.

Normally amiable, Clarry could feel rage burning up inside him as he looked down into the sneering face on the dustman. 'You are a nasty wee man,' said Clarry. 'I've given you a warning, but it would be a grand day for the village if you were killed.' He turned and walked away and then turned back at the garden gate. 'By God, man, I could kill you myself.'

And, followed by the sound of Fergus's jeering laughter, he walked away.

Clarry walked only as far as the waterfront. He leaned on the wall and stared down into the summer-blue waters of the sea loch. A yacht sailed past, heading for the open sea. He could hear people laughing and chattering on board, see the white sails billowing out before a stiff breeze. He suddenly wanted to see

Martha. He turned his back to the wall, feeling the warmth of the stone through his uniform. While Hamish Macbeth watered his sheep and then returned to the police station to do some paperwork and wondered what was keeping Clarry, Clarry stayed where he was. Perhaps Martha might appear, perhaps she might go to the general store for something.

With monumental patience, Clarry stayed where he was until the sun began to sink down behind the mountains. She might come down to the village to buy something. Patel, who ran the general store, like all good Asian shopkeepers, stayed open late.

Suddenly he saw her hurrying down the lane that led to the waterfront, carrying a shopping basket. He went to meet her.

'Oh, Mr Graham!' exclaimed Martha. Her hand fluttered up to one cheek to cover a bruise.

'He's been hitting you!' said Clarry.

'Oh, no,' said Martha. 'Silly of me. I walked into a door.'

'You walked into a fist,' said Clarry. 'You've got to turn him in.'

'I can't,' said Martha, tears starting to her eyes.

'Now, then, I didnae mean to upset you, lassie,' said Clarry. 'Let me help you with the shopping.'

'I can manage. Fergus wants a bottle of whisky.'

'Drinking again? That's bad.'

'At least he'll wander off somewhere, and I'll get a bit of peace,' said Martha. They walked into the store together.

'Buy him the cheap stuff,' said Clarry.

'No, he wants Grouse.'

'Let me pay for it.'

'No, that would not be fitting.'

'I came up to your place to warn him. Steady, now!' Clarry grasped the bottle of whisky which Martha had nearly dropped.

'What about?' she asked.

'He's creating bad feeling in the village. He could be in danger. God, I could kill him myself.'

Jessie Currie, at the shelves on the other side from where they were talking and screened from their view, listened avidly.

'I'd better hurry,' said Martha. 'He'll start wondering what's keeping me.'

'I'll walk you back a bit of the way,' said Clarry. Curious village eyes watched them as Martha paid for the whisky and then they walked out of the shop together.

Later that evening, Hamish was barely soothed by the plate of beef Wellington that Clarry slid under his nose. He had been called out to a burglary in the nearby town of Braikie, and he wondered after he had completed his investigations what the point was of having a

31

constable who was so supremely uninterested in police matters. But he noticed a change had come over Clarry. His face seemed harder.

'So what happened with Fergus?' asked Hamish.

Clarry told him, ending up with bursting out, 'He's been beating his wife again. I tell you, sir, I've a damn good mind to resign from the force and give that bastard the beating he deserves.'

Hamish stared in wonder at the nearly untouched food on Clarry's plate and then at the angry gleam in the normally placid constable's eyes.

He leaned back in his chair. 'Of all the things to happen,' said Hamish. 'You haff gone and fallen in love wi' the dustman's wife.'

Clarry stared at him. Then his eyes lit up and his round face glowed. 'Is this love, sir?'

'Yes, but she's married and this iss the small village. Eat your food, man, and forget her. I'll deal wi' Fergus myself tomorrow.'

'How?'

'We haff our methods, Watson.'

But Hamish Macbeth was getting seriously worried. The transformation of the constable had sharpened his wits. Fergus must be made to see sense.

Even if it meant giving him a taste of what he had been giving his wife.

* * *

The following day was collection day, and Lochdubh rose to find the rubbish uncollected. It was a warm, close day, and the midges, those Highland mosquitoes, were out in force.

Fergus had disappeared before but never on collection days. But he had become so hated in the village that nobody cared much, with the exception of Hamish Macbeth. Still, even Hamish thought, like everyone else, that surely Fergus was lying drunk somewhere up on the moors. But after a day went by without any sight of him, Hamish's uneasiness deepened into dread.

'If something's happened to him, we'd better find out soon,' said Hamish to Clarry. 'We'll split up. You search around the village, and I'll take the Land Rover and go up on the moors.'

Clarry set off. As he questioned villager after villager, he began to share some of Hamish's trepidation. 'I hope he's dead,' said Archie Maclean, pausing in the repair of a fishing net. 'And if the wee bastard isnnae, I'll help him on his way.'

Everyone else seemed to share Archie's sentiments. Clarry walked along the harbour to where the workmen were busy renovating the hotel. None of them had seen Fergus but one volunteered the information that the boss had arrived. Curious to see this hotel owner, Clarry made his way into the foyer of the hotel, where two men were unwrapping a massive crystal chandelier. 'Boss around?' he asked.

'In the office over there,' said one, jerking his thumb in the direction of a frosted-glass door. Clarry ambled across the foyer and opened the door. A slim red-headed woman was sitting behind a computer. 'Yes, Officer?'

'Is the boss in?' asked Clarry.

'May I ask what the nature of your inquiry is?'

'The village dustman has gone missing.'

A faint look of amusement crossed her beautiful face. 'I am sure Mr Ionides, who has just arrived here, cannot know anything about a dustman.'

The door to the inner office opened and a small, neat, well-barbered man appeared. He had thick, dark brown hair and liquid brown eyes. He was in his shirt sleeves and carried a sheaf of papers. He radiated energy. His eyes fell on the large uniformed figure of Clarry.

'What is a policeman doing here?' he asked. His voice was only faintly accented.

'I've come about our dustman. He's missing.'

'And what has that got to do with me?'

Clarry shifted awkwardly from foot to foot. 'I thought you might have heard something, sir.'

'No.'

Ionides and his secretary calmly surveyed Clarry, who began to shuffle backwards towards the door. 'Just thought I would ask,' said Clarry.

They continued to watch him in silence as he turned and opened the door and went out. Phew, he thought, mopping his brow outside the door. What an odd pair.

He realized once he was outside the hotel that he had been delaying going to see Martha. He somehow didn't want to go to that cottage and find Fergus at home. The villagers were right. The man didn't deserve to live. It did not strike Clarry as odd that so many people would wish the death of a mere dustman. Dustmen who fail to collect rubbish can arouse deep passions, and dustmen who leave nasty green notes to explain why the rubbish is not being collected can drive the meekest to open hatred. High council taxes had made everyone aware that they were paying for a service they just weren't getting.

Clarry walked more quickly now as he neared Fergus's cottage. As he approached, his eyes took in the broken guttering and the blistered paint on the windows, and he mentally repaired all the damage.

He knocked on the door and waited. Johnny answered, his little face lighting up when he saw Clarry. 'Mum's out in the back garden,' he said. Clarry removed his peaked cap and tucked it under his arm. He followed the boy through the dark little living room where the children were watching television. Probably too frightened to play outside in case Dad comes home, he thought.

Martha was hanging sheets out to dry in the back garden. A breeze blew strands of hair across her face. 'Let me do that,' said Clarry, taking a sheet from her. 'Heard from that man of yours?'

'Not a word,' said Martha. 'He's never missed a collection day before.'

'Is he in his uniform? That green would make him easy to spot.'

'No, he was in a white shirt, tie and jacket. He took that bottle of whisky from me and walked off out of the house.'

Together they lifted up sheets and pinned them along the line. Martha paused to pass a weary hand over her brow. 'Goodness, it's hot.'

'You and the children should be out on a day like this,' said Clarry.

'Fergus might be back any moment,' said Martha. 'I must say I sometimes look down at the loch on a day like this and think it would be nice to go out on a boat and get a bit of cool air.'

'That's the last sheet,' said Clarry. 'Well, why not?'

'We couldn't. What if Fergus comes home?'

'Then you can say you were out wi' me looking for him. Come on. Get the kids.'

Curious village eyes watched the procession made up of Clarry and Martha, the children and the baby in the pram as they walked down to the waterfront.

'What's going on, going on?' asked Jessie Currie, standing outside Patel's store. 'Have they found him, found him?'

'Shouldn't think so,' said Nessie. 'Martha's laughing. Never heard her laugh before.'

Both sisters, the sun glinting on their thick spectacles, watched as Clarry stopped to speak to Archie Maclean. 'He's giving him money,' said Nessie. 'Now they're getting into that rowboat. Michty me, doesn't that policeman have any work to do?'

'It's Hamish Macbeth, that's who it is, who it is,' said Jessie. 'Corrupted him in no time at all, no time at all.'

They watched while Clarry pushed off and then jumped in, the boat swaying dangerously under his weight. Then he picked up the oars and began to row off towards the centre of the loch. The children began to laugh at something. Martha sat in the bow, the baby on her lap, smiling at Clarry.

'Trouble's coming out of that,' said Nessie. 'Mark my words.'

Hamish Macbeth was tired and hot and thirsty. He had searched across the moors all day without finding Fergus or coming across anyone who had seen him.

At last he drove slowly back towards Loch-dubh and then on impulse turned and drove up towards the Tommel Castle Hotel. The castle had been built in the last century by a beer baron with a taste for gothic architecture.

He parked and walked into the hotel. Priscilla came out of the hotel office and came forward to meet him.

'You look exhausted,' she said. 'Like a drink?'

'A long cold drink o' iced fizzy water would be grand.'

'Come into the bar, and I'll get it for you.' Hamish followed her into the bar. She was wearing a lime green cotton shirt worn loose over a pair of cream shorts. Her long tanned legs ended in low-heeled strapped sandals. A shaft of late sunlight striking through the mullioned windows of the bar turned her golden hair into an aureole.

Priscilla asked the barman for an orange juice for herself and a fizzy water for Hamish. They carried their drinks over to a table.

'What have you been up to?' asked Priscilla.

'Looking for our missing dustman.'

'I hope you find him. We had to pay a contractor to come over from Strathbane and pick up ours. Surely he's just drunk again.'

'Well, normally that would be the case. But the wee man has caused such hatred in the village wi' his bullying and his silly green uniform, I'm frightened someone lost their temper and hit him too hard.'

'You're getting carried away, Hamish. Just think of everyone in Lochdubh. They always curse Fergus, some of the crofters might rough him up, but no one is going to kill him.'

Hamish took a gulp of water and stretched out his long legs. 'That's better. To tell the truth, Priscilla, I still fear someone may have gone too far. He's a wife beater and, if I'd got him on his own, I might have been tempted to give him a bit of his own medicine.'

'That's not your style, Hamish!'

'Look, we're a laid-back, easygoing lot, and we don't like this wee monster disrupting our lives.'

'Someone said he used to be an accountant. Is that true?'

'I believe so, before the drink got him. I'll put in a report tonight to Strathbane head-quarters and then one to the council. We'll need a replacement.'

'That'll be hard to find.'

'Not in the least. The crofters all have some sort of part-time job, especially since the price they've been getting for sheep has slumped. Callum McSween up on the Braikie road is a nice man and could do wi' a bit o' extra money.'

'Never mind, Hamish. It's the bad atmos-phere Fergus has created in the village that's getting to you. Then this warm weather makes all the uncollected rubbish smell so high that it gets on people's nerves as well.'

Hamish finished his glass of water. 'I'd best be getting back. Maybe Clarry's found something out.'

'How's he getting on?'

'Oh, he's a nice chap and a grand cook. I don't mind so much just now. Things are pretty quiet apart from a burglary over at Braikie and this Fergus business.' He stood up. 'You going back to London soon?'

'I'll be staying on for a bit. Father's worried sick about this new hotel taking our custom away.'

'Aye, well, maybe we'll have a meal some night.'

Priscilla looked down at her glass. 'I'll let you know. I've got a friend coming up from London tomorrow.'

A man friend, thought Hamish, looking at her bent head.

'Yes, let me know,' he said and walked off, feeling depressed.

He drove down to the police station and swung the Land Rover into the short drive beside the building. It was only when he cut the engine that he heard the noise. Music was belting out from the police station, disco music, loud and throbbing; so loud the police station seemed to be vibrating.

Instead of walking in the kitchen door as usual, he went quietly round to the front and looked in the living room window. Clarry was dancing, surrounded by laughing children. He was bopping about and waving his arms. Martha was watching them, her face lit up with amusement.

Hamish retreated quietly. He knew Clarry had no right to invite guests to the police station without permission and no right to throw a party. He should march in there like a good police officer and break up the party.

But instead he walked back along the waterfront to the Italian restaurant. He felt in his bones that something bad had happened. Let Martha enjoy herself while she could.

Nessie Curry carried a kitchen chair out to the wheelie bin beside the cottage she shared with her twin sister, Jessie. She placed the chair beside the bin and climbed up on it, holding a bag of rubbish. Fergus would just need to put up with the bottles and cans, for all the little plastic boxes were full. She raised the lid of the bin and then gagged at the smell and clung to the bin for support as she hurriedly dropped the lid.

She retreated back into the kitchen. 'Oh, Jessie,' she said. 'There's the most terrible smell coming from our wheelie bin. What did you put in it?'

'All the papers and bottles and stuff I couldn't get into thae wee boxes, wee boxes,' said Jessie. 'I haven't put anything in there for a couple of days, couple of days.'

'What about food scraps?'

'They went to the compost heap and the rest to Mrs Docherty's hens next door, hens next door.'

'Then someone's put something nasty in ours.'

'Call Hamish Macbeth, Hamish Macbeth.'

'I saw him pass the window an hour ago. He's probably gone to the Italian's. I'll just go along and get him. It's his job to look for nasty things.'

Hamish was just finishing his meal when Nessie arrived. He listened to her tale of the smelly bin and said, 'I'll be along in a minute. Have a torch ready. It'll save going back to the station.'

Hamish paid for his meal and then walked out. It was a warm, balmy evening. The reflections of stars shimmered on the black waters of the loch.

He walked round to the side door of the Currie sisters' cottage. Nessie was waiting for him with a large electric torch. 'Let's see what you've got,' said Hamish, taking the torch from her.

The minute he opened the lid of the bin and the horrible smell engulfed him, he felt a lump of ice settling in his stomach. He knew that smell.

Tall as he was, he nonetheless climbed up on the chair and shone the strong beam down into the bin. The dead face of Fergus Macleod stared up at him. Hamish took out a handkerchief and put it over his hand and turned the head slightly. There was a large gaping wound in the back of it. There was a sudden sickening sound of buzzing. The light from the torch was awakening the flies, fat bluebottles. He slammed down the lid and climbed down from the chair.

Nessie and Jessie were both standing together now, staring at him in the starlight.

'What is it?' asked Nessie.

'Fergus. It's Fergus. Don't touch anything, ladies. It's murder.'

Chapter Three

Earth to earth, ashes to ashes, dust to dust.
— Book of Common Prayer

The next day dawned, still and pale and milky, all colour bleached out of the landscape. The striped police tape hung outside the Currie sisters' cottage. Little groups of villagers stood outside, as motionless as the heavy air.

Clarry stood on duty, his usually cherubic face heavy and sad. The party of last night seemed light years away. Hamish had sent him to break the news to Martha. She had shrunk from him, her eyes dilated with shock. Mrs Wellington, the minister's wife, alerted by the news which had spread like wildfire through Lochdubh, had arrived to sit with Martha.

Clarry would have liked to talk, to banish the fright he saw in Martha's eyes which seemed to stem from something other than the horror at learning of her husband's death. He had an uneasy feeling that Martha, upset by the news, might think that he, Clarry, had

45

bumped off her husband. Or was it something else? Could *she* have done it? He shook his head like a bull plagued by flies. That was ridiculous. He wondered how Hamish was getting on along at the police station. Detective Chief Inspector Blair had arrived.

Blair was the bane of Hamish's life. He was a thick, vulgar, heavyset Glaswegian who loathed Hamish and did not bother to hide his loathing.

He was sitting behind the desk in the police station office, flanked by his usual sidekicks, Detectives Anderson and Macnab.

'Now, from a preliminary questioning of the folks around here,' began Blair, 'there was one hell of a party going on in this station last night.'

'This is also my home as well as a police station. I am allowed to throw a party,' said Hamish defensively.

'But it wasnae your party, was it?' demanded Blair with a triumphant leer. 'It was that fat, useless copper o' yours. And who is he boogieing with? None other than Martha Macleod. Furthermore, Mrs Macleod's neighbours heard Clarry Graham shouting at Fergus that he would kill him.'

'A lot of people in the village have been overheard saying they would kill Fergus. It means nothing,' said Hamish.

'We'll see aboot that. As far as I am concerned, Graham is a suspect so you get along there and send him along here.'

Hamish rose to his feet. 'All right.'

'All right, what?'

'All right, sir,' said Hamish wearily. He craved sleep. He had been up all night.

He went out and walked along to the Curries' cottage. 'Blair wants to see you,' he said to Clarry.

'Why?'

'At the moment, you're suspect number one.'

'That's daft!'

'Maybe. But run along and get it over with.'

Clarry walked off just as the police pathologist, Mr Sinclair, appeared round the side of the house. 'What's the verdict?' asked Hamish.

'The body's being moved to Strathbane for further examination,' said Sinclair. 'He was struck a smashing blow on the back of the head with something like a hammer and put in the bin.'

'When?'

'Can't tell at the moment. I would hazard a guess that it was maybe a couple of days ago.'

'Could a woman have done it?'

'Easily. But although the man was small and slight, it would take a powerful woman to get him into that bin without tipping it over.'

They stood aside as two men in white overalls carried out Fergus in a body bag laid on a stretcher. They looked impatiently up and down the waterfront and then one put his fingers in his mouth and sent out a shrill whistle. An ambulance came cruising slowly up.

'Sorry. We were just getting a cup of coffee,' said the ambulance man. He jumped down with his partner and opened the back doors. Fergus's body was lifted inside.

Hamish felt a pang of pity for Fergus. He had been an awful man, but the sheer indifference in the way his body was shovelled in and borne off went to his heart.

In all his easygoing life, Clarry had never before thought of leaving the police force. But he had never been one of Blair's targets before. As Blair hammered into him over a sheaf of reports about the party and the boat expedition, Clarry could feel a rare rage mounting in him.

When Blair paused for breath, Clarry said, 'Are you charging me with anything, sir?'

'Not yet.'

'This is police harassment,' said Clarry.

'Whit! You're a policeman yourself.'

'I want a lawyer.'

'Don't be daft.'

'It was my day off when I entertained Mrs Macleod and the children,' said Clarry, hoping Hamish would back him up on that one. 'I can do what I like with my free time. It's a coincidence that the poor woman's man got murdered.'

'Oh, aye?' sneered Blair. 'And it's just a coin-cidence, is it, that you were heard saying you'd kill the man?'

'More than me said that,' said Clarry, defi-ant. 'Fergus had been beating that wife of his. It was enough to make the blood of any decent man boil.'

'Did she make an official complaint?'

'No, sir.'

'Then it was none of your business. For all you know, she might have deserved a beating. You Highlanders are all crazy,' said Blair, who was a Glaswegian.

'That remark is offensive,' said Clarry, sud-denly calm. 'I'm going to report that remark to the Race Relations Board. Discrimination against Highlanders. Racial slurs. And while I'm at it, sir, I'll tell them that you think a woman deserves a beating.'

'You do that, and I'll have ye out o' the force.'

'And by the time I've finished with *you*, I'll have you out of the force.'

Blair stared at Clarry's now impassive face in baffled fury. He had no doubt the Race Relations Board would listen to this idiot's complaint. Recently, along with dealing with cases brought by Pakistanis, Indians, Africans and Jamaicans, they had been handling well-publicized cases from English residents in Scotland complaining about racial discrimina-tion. And if that remark of his about Martha

Macleod deserving a beating should come out ...

'Look, laddie, maybe I was a bit hasty. You go and question some of the folk and find out if anyone saw anything.'

Clarry stalked off. Blair mopped his brow. He turned and caught the grin on Jimmy Anderson's face. 'You!' he howled. 'Get up to that Mrs Macleod and question her.'

Jimmy Anderson stopped on his way to talk to Hamish and gleefully told Hamish about Clarry's confrontation with Blair. 'Good for old Clarry,' said Hamish, amazed. 'Where are you off to?'

'To interview the widow.'

'Let me know what you get, Jimmy.'

'Aye, well, get some whisky in. I don't think Blair will be hanging around much longer.'

'He hasn't met Mrs Fleming yet, has he?'

'Who's she?'

'The environment woman from Strathbane who put Fergus in a stupid green uniform and put all these bins about the place. She'll be here any moment, if I'm not mistaken.'

'See you later.'

Jimmy walked off. Hamish took out his mobile phone and rang Callum McSween. 'Listen, Callum,' he said, 'have you heard the dustman's got himself murdered?'

'Aye, it was on the radio this morning.'

'Like the job?'

'I could do wi' the money, Hamish, and that's a fact.'

'I'll be sending a Mrs Fleming from Strathbane Council along to see you. She's the one who'll be doing the hiring. I think the silly biddy wants to get herself in the newspapers by making Lochdubh an environmental friendly place, so all you have to do is go along with it. Tell her what a great idea all those damn bins are.'

'I won't have to wear that green uniform, will I?'

'I can't see them running to the expense of another horror. I'll make sure Fergus is buried in it.'

'Grand, Hamish.'

'I can't promise. Oh, here she comes.'

Hamish rang off and tucked the phone in his pocket just as Mrs Fleming drove up.

'I heard the news,' she said, lowering the car window. 'This is dreadful.'

'That it is,' said Hamish seriously. 'And rubbish all over the village. You'll need to get another man on it right away.'

'But who?'

'There's a crofter about a mile along the Braikie Road, Callum McSween, good worker, hot on the environment. He could start today.'

'I'll go directly.' Hamish gave her directions. Then she asked, 'Who is in charge of the case?'

'Detective Chief Inspector Blair. You'll find him at the police station. But I'd get to Callum first.'

Callum McSween was dressed in a crisp white shirt and flannels with knife-edged creases when Mrs Fleming's car drove up. His wife, Mary, had quickly cleaned the living room and was in the kitchen making a pot of fresh coffee.

Callum answered the door to Mrs Fleming. He was a very tall, well-built man with a craggy face permanently tanned with working outdoors.

'I am Mrs Fleming from Strathbane Council,' she said. 'Do you mind if I come in? I heard you might be prepared to take on the job of environment officer for Lochdubh.'

Callum, affecting surprise, invited her in.

His smiling wife came into the croft house living room bearing a tray with a pot of coffee, cups and homemade shortbread.

'I first must ask you if you understand what I have been trying to do in Lochdubh,' began Mrs Fleming when she had been served with coffee.

'I think you are out to make an example of Lochdubh,' said Callum. He leaned forward, his face serious. 'If it works, you can get it into the newspapers and on television as an example to other villages. And I can tell you,

I am all for that. There's a real pleasure in seeing a clean place.'

Mrs Fleming smiled at him. She mentally judged that he would look well on television. 'There would be the matter of a uniform, Mr McSween.'

Callum repressed a shudder. 'As to that, missus, I haff been thinking that maybe white overalls would be fine. You must want to save a bit o' money. I mean, poor Fergus's outfit must have cost a mint. But the white overalls would look just grand.'

'I'll see to it. Ye-es, I can see white overalls.' In Mrs Fleming's busy mind, the cameras rolled. She raised her hands and made a frame of them and studied Callum through it. 'When would you be able to start?'

'Right away.

'Good. I will get that policeman in Lochdubh to give you the keys to the truck. As to salary . . .'

She named a figure which made Callum's eyes blink rapidly. He would never have dreamed a dustman could earn that much. He had an appointment with the bank manager on the following morning. The bank was trying to call in his loan, and he had been terrified of losing his croft house.

They amicably discussed the details. Then Mrs Fleming took her leave. Mary McSween, who had heard the size of the salary, just restrained herself from dropping a curtsy as Mrs Fleming majestically swept out.

Callum dialled 1-4-7-1 and then dialled 3 and got connected to Hamish's mobile phone. 'I've got the job, Hamish,' he shouted.

Hamish held the phone away from his ear. 'You didnae need to phone, Callum, wi' a voice like that. You could have just stood outside your front door.'

'It's great, Hamish. I tell you, man, if there's anything I can ever do for you, let me know.'

'Just keep your eyes and ears open and let me know if you hear anything interesting.'

'I'll do that. Oh, I need the keys to the truck.'

'I'll go get them. Come by the station this afternoon.'

Hamish decided there was not much point anyone standing outside the Curries' cottage any longer. The body had gone. The forensic team had finished their work and had left, taking the bin with them wrapped up in plastic.

Hamish walked up towards Martha's cottage. He met Jimmy Anderson on the way. 'How did you get on?'

'Nothing much,' said Jimmy. 'Mrs Macleod began to cry and that big tweedy woman, Mrs Wellington, sent me off with a flea in my ear. What sort of woman wears tweed in this weather?'

'Mrs Wellington.'

'So what are you up to?'

'Going to collect the keys to the rubbish truck. Forensic don't want it, do they?'

'No, the neighbours say the truck was never moved from outside of the house.'

'Fine. Call by later when you get rid of Blair.'

'He doesn't want this case, Hamish. He was working on some drugs bust, and he wants to get back to it.'

'Let's hope he does before he starts arresting everyone in the village.'

Hamish walked on. He saw Mrs Wellington walking towards him before she saw him. He leapt over a hedge and crouched behind it until he heard her go past. Then he leapt nimbly back over and walked to Martha's cottage. Martha was keeping to the old tradition. All the curtains in the cottage were closed tight.

Hamish walked up the path and knocked on the door. There was a silence. He waited and knocked again. At last he tried the handle and opened the door and called, 'Mrs Macleod.'

'Go away!' shouted a boy's voice.

'It's me, Hamish Macbeth.'

Johnny appeared. 'Oh, it is yourself, Mr Macbeth. The reporters have been around.'

'Is your mother in?'

'Come ben.'

Hamish walked into the living room. Martha was sitting there, dull-eyed, the baby on her lap.

Hamish removed his cap and sat down

opposite her. Johnny joined the other children on the sofa. Their faces were white in the gloom.

'I know you've got the curtains drawn as a mark of respect,' said Hamish gently. 'But it's not good for the children. Do you mind if I let some daylight in here?'

'Do what you like,' whispered Martha.

Hamish jerked back the curtains.

Then he took five pounds out of his wallet and gave it to Johnny. 'Take yourselves down to Patel's and get yourself some ice cream. Put the bairn in the pram and take it with you. It's no good to be locked up in here. Don't speak to any reporters.'

Johnny looked at his mother, who nodded. Johnny took the baby from her and the children filed out of the room.

Hamish studied Martha's white face and wide frightened eyes. He said, 'You must be feeling a great deal of guilt.'

'I didn't do it!'

'But you wanted him gone, but not in this way. You're relieved and ashamed of being relieved. You're frightened that whoever did this might come for you. That won't happen. It was Fergus who caused bad blood in this village, not you. You're worried about Clarry. Clarry when he wasn't with me was either with you or in full view of the village. Can you remember exactly what happened the evening Fergus disappeared?'

'He got a phone call and became very excited,' said Martha.

'Good, that's a start. We'll check your phone records. What time would that be?'

'About six o'clock. He asked me to go and get him some whisky. I couldn't help it. I said, what about your job? He told me to shut my mouth. He said there was more to life than being a dustman. I went down to Patel's. I met Clarry and talked a bit and then went back with the whisky. He had a couple of drams and then he said he was going out. He put the whisky bottle in his pocket. He must have been going somewhere in the village because he didn't take the truck.'

'Aye, but when your man had the drink taken, he'd often wander up on the moors, so why would you think it was somewhere in the village?'

'I think he must have been going to meet someone.'

'Why?'

'He put a clean white shirt on and a tie and his jacket. He liked his white shirts to be very white. That's why I thought someone might have seen him, even in the gloaming.'

'So when he didn't return, weren't you worried about him?'

'No. Any time before he had started to drink, he would disappear for a few days.'

'But you thought he had gone to see someone.'

Martha burst out with, 'Don't you see? I was just so damn glad he had gone, I didn't think. I lived for his disappearances.'

'Did he often get phone calls?'

'No. He wasn't popular.'

'I think that'll do for now.' Hamish looked around the bleak cottage. 'Have they been to search his things?'

'Yes, the detectives were here, looking for letters or papers. But there wasn't anything.'

'I'll arrange for someone to come and help you clear out his stuff. Best to get rid of the reminders.'

'Thank you.'

Hamish said goodbye and left. He made his way back to the police station. He walked into the kitchen. Clarry was sitting bouncing Martha's baby on his knee while the children sat around eating ice cream.

Hamish addressed Johnny. 'You'd all better get home right away and look after your mother. She'll be beginning to wonder where you are, and I don't want her pestered by reporters.'

Clarry carried the baby out to the pram. He would have gone with them, but Hamish ordered him to stay. When the children had gone, he said, 'Clarry, you've caused enough gossip. Leave the poor woman alone for a bit.'

'She needs help!'

'I'll get her help. Now I've got to make a phone call.'

Hamish went through to the police office and dialled Strathbane headquarters. He asked to be put through to Blair and to his surprise the phone call was answered by Superintendent Peter Daviot.

'I was trying to reach Mr Blair,' said Hamish.

'I happened to be in the detectives' room when the phone rang. There's no one here at the moment. What's it about?'

Hamish said, 'I had a word with Martha Macleod, the dustman's widow.' He told Daviot about the phone call, ending with, 'So I thought headquarters could get on to tracing that call right away.'

'Good work, Hamish. I'll let Blair know.'

Back in the kitchen, Clarry was producing out of the oven a steaming casserole of boeuf bourguignon.

'Smells great,' said Hamish, 'but I've got to go out for a bit, and, when I get back, until we hear from Blair, we may as well start questioning everyone in the village, even if they have been questioned already.'

He made his way to Dr Brodie's house and knocked at the kitchen door. Angela, the doctor's wife, answered. 'Oh, come in, Hamish. Terrible business about Fergus.'

Hamish followed her into the kitchen. 'I've come about Martha,' he said. 'Perhaps you and some of the other women could call on her and give her a hand clearing out Fergus's old stuff.'

'I was going to do that anyway. You'd best have a word with the Currie sisters.'

'Why? Are they terribly upset over the murder?'

Angela pushed a wisp of hair away from her thin face. 'It's not that, Hamish. It's Clarry.'

'What about him?'

'Jessie overheard him in Patel's on the evening Fergus disappeared threatening to kill him. Martha's neighbours heard him before that threatening to kill Fergus. You'd better shut them up.'

'Like I told you, Clarry's already been grilled by Blair and wonder upon wonders, he hasnae been arrested. And talking about shutting people up, I'd best go round to the Currie sisters.'

'What?' demanded Nessie Currie wrathfully. 'Us gossiping? I thought it was too much to hope that a lazy loon like you might actually call to see how we were.'

'The situation is this,' said Hamish severely. 'I sent Clarry up to Martha Macleod to look after her. If he wasn't with her, he was with me.'

'Huh,' snorted Nessie, 'and why would she need looking after?'

'This was afore the murder. Her husband had been beating her.'

'Beating her?' echoed Jessie. 'But herself always said she was clumsy, was clumsy.'

'Well, he was beating her, and she's a poor soul in need of friends. Angela Brodie's getting some of the women together to help Martha clear out Fergus's things.'

'And I suppose you want us to help?' demanded Nessie.

'It would be a Christian act.'

'But did I not hear Clarry Graham saying he would kill Fergus, would kill Fergus!' exclaimed Jessie.

'Come on. Half the village must have been heard saying they would kill Fergus.'

'And he was beating her?' said Nessie.

'That he was. Can you imagine what her life was like, ladies?'

'So she must be feeling glad that he's dead.'

'Dead,' echoed her sister.

'It'll be a long time afore she feels that way. She feels guilt, anger, remorse and fear. She'll be worried sick about money.'

'She could get a job, get a job,' said Jessie.

'How? She's got four young children.'

'Eileen, who works up at the Tommel Castle Hotel, told me she has an arrangement with the other workers. They work shifts, and the one that isn't working at a specific time looks after the children of the others,' said Nessie.

'I'll be looking into that. So you'll help?'

'Yes,' said Nessie. 'Only, if more women stayed unmarried like us, there'd be less grief in the world. And by the way, the new school-teacher is arriving in a couple of days. I hope you're not going to chase her like you did the last one.'

'Good evening,' said Hamish firmly, and made his escape.

So Maisie, the previous schoolteacher, had decided not to come back. Hamish wondered what the new one would be like. Then he remembered Priscilla's friend who would have arrived by now. He wished he had some lady friend to show Priscilla that he definitely did not care any more who she invited or what she did.

But curiosity overcame him. He returned to the police station and got in the Land Rover. Before he switched on the engine, he heard Lugs scrabbling at the kitchen door. He sighed and got down from the Land Rover and opened the door. 'Come on, boy,' he said. 'I've been neglecting you.' When he straightened up after fastening a leash around the dog's neck, he saw an empty plate on the kitchen table with a note beside it. It was from Clarry. 'I heard you coming so I left your dinner on the table.'

Hamish looked down at his dog, who licked his lips and hung his head. 'You're full o' boeuf bourguignon you lousy animal.' Lugs looked up at him imploringly out of his odd blue eyes.

'Oh, come on anyway,' said Hamish crossly. 'But if you go on like this, you'll be as fat as Clarry.' Hamish lifted his dog into the passenger seat, got in himself and drove off.

It took him just five minutes to drive to the Tommel Castle Hotel. The car park was full. He walked into the hotel foyer with Lugs on a leash. He looked in the bar and hurriedly retreated. It was full of journalists. One was trying to balance a glass of whisky on his nose and the others were cheering him on. Hamish retreated and then looked in the dining room. Priscilla was sitting at a table with a tall, good-looking man. She looked up and saw Hamish and waved him over.

Her companion, advertising executive Jerry Darcy, was a kind and amiable man. But the sight of the tall, gangly policeman with the flaming red hair leading an odd mongrel with big ears and blue eyes was too much for him. He began to laugh helplessly.

'Jerry, please,' admonished Priscilla. 'This is our policeman, Hamish Macbeth. Hamish, Jerry Darcy.'

Jerry wiped his streaming eyes and got courteously to his feet. 'Something amusing you?' demanded Hamish.

'Sorry,' said Jerry with a grin. 'It was you and that dog.'

'And what iss up with my dog?'

'It's an odd-looking animal, you must admit.'

'There iss nothing whateffer up wi' my dog,' said Hamish, furious because he felt ridiculous, furious because Priscilla's beau was handsome and well-dressed.

Lugs, sensing his master's rage, grabbed hold of the tablecloth and began to back away, pulling it. Wineglasses and two plates of food tumbled on to the floor.

'Lugs!' shouted Hamish, his face red with embarrassment. 'I'm sorry, Priscilla. I'd better take him away. I'll talk to you tomorrow.'

Hamish dragged Lugs back into the foyer, only to find himself surrounded by reporters. To all their questions, he said, 'Call Detective Chief Inspector Blair at Strathbane,' and made his escape.

Once in the Land Rover, he sat there for a few moments, cursing Lugs and cursing his own bad temper. Lugs let out a pathetic little whimper, and Hamish patted the animal's rough coat. 'It wasnae your fault, laddie. But he shouldnae have laughed at me.'

Hamish had set the alarm and woke early and roused Clarry. 'I want you to go to the Currie sisters and take them through their story again. I mean, that pair are always peering through their net curtains at what's going on. I'll start with the fisherman. Blair'll be here soon so we'd best get out and about. I gather you got out of being arrested. How?'

Clarry told him how and Hamish laughed and laughed. 'Man, I'd have liked to see Blair's face when you threatened him with the Race Relations Board. Now let's get a move on.'

Hamish headed for the harbour. He saw Callum McSween, who said he was ready to start work. Hamish gave him the keys to the rubbish truck. Callum walked off. Hamish saw Archie, sitting disconsolately on the harbour wall.

'Nowhere to drink?' asked Hamish, who knew the fisherman usually headed for the Lochdubh bar after a night's work.

'That foreigner bought it,' said Archie, 'and he iss going to turn it into the gift shop. So I'm stuck out here in the open where the wife can find me.'

'Archie, you didn't like Fergus much, did you?'

'No, that I didn't, and nobody else did either. We didnae notice him much until he got that stupid uniform and started bossing us all around. But none of us would ha' touched him, Hamish. You know that.'

'Any gossip? Anyone see him around?'

'Well, there was one odd thing. One person seemed to like him.'

'And who was that?'

'Josie Darling.'

'Her? She's getting all ready for her wedding.'

'Aye, she's taken time off work, too.'

65

Hamish thought hard. Josie was young and frivolous. She lived with her mother in a cottage up a lane at the back of the new hotel. 'I'll go and see her.'

He walked towards Josie's cottage, glancing up at the sky. It was a milky blue but there was a dampness in the breeze on his cheek. Rain coming soon, he thought.

He turned over in his mind what he knew about Josie. She worked in a bank in Strathbane and was engaged to someone from Inverness. Her father was dead. Her mother worked as a maid at the Tommel Castle Hotel. She planned to live in Inverness after her marriage. A big wedding was to be held in the Church of Scotland in Lochdubh and, as was the tradition at Highland weddings, the whole village was going. The wedding was to be in two weeks' time.

He knocked on the cottage door and then turned around and surveyed the view while he waited for someone to answer it. Down on the waterfront, he could see the white-overalled figure of Callum McSween working busily. He turned back as the door opened.

Josie stood there. She was a small girl with dyed blonde hair and a pug face. She had large, rather protruding eyes. She was wearing a short skirt which displayed fat legs to disadvantage and a low-cut blouse. Those eyes goggled when she saw Hamish.

'What is it?' she asked harshly.

'Can I come in?'

She backed away reluctantly. He followed her into the living room. On a coffee table were many glossy magazines, *Brides*, *Your Wedding*, *Hair and Beauty*.

'Getting ready for the wedding?' asked Hamish.

'Oh, that. I'm not having it in Lochdubh.'

'Why not? Everyone's been looking forward to it.'

'Murdo wants to have it in Inverness.'

'Murdo being your fiancé?'

'Yes.'

'I thought the wedding was usually held in the bride's parish.'

'Yes, but I've only got Mother. Murdo's got loads of relatives, so we thought it would be more reasonable to have it in Inverness. Anyway, I'm sick of this place.'

'Lochdubh?'

'Where else?'

'Why?'

'It's so provincial,' said Josie.

Hamish privately thought that Josie was hardly the picture of sophistication.

'Anyway,' said Josie, 'is that why you came? To ask about the wedding?'

'No, it's about Fergus.'

'The dustman? What about him?'

'I believe you were friendly with him.'

'Och, no. I just gave the wee man a cup of tea from time to time. That way he took all our rubbish.'

'Did you like him?'

Again that sort of false grande dame air. 'He was just a dustman. I sometimes chat to the postman as well.'

'So is there anything you can tell me about him? Did he look frightened about anything? Did he say anyone was out to get him?'

'No, he just said they were all bastards, and he hated them. He didn't say whether anyone hated him.'

'Well, if you remember anything, let me know.'

Hamish said goodbye. But as he walked down from the cottage, he thought, she's lying. There's something there. I'll let her think she's safe, and then I'll go back. I'll try Mrs Darling up at the hotel.

He went to the police station to collect the Land Rover and was confronted by a raging Detective Chief Inspector Blair. He pointed to a torn trouser leg. 'Look what your dog did!' he shouted.

'Did you just walk into the station?' asked Hamish.

'Yes!'

'Well, there you are. Lugs is a guard dog.'

'You'll pay for this.' Blair was in a foul temper. Peter Daviot had called him in and had told him that Hamish had secured an excellent interview with the widow Macleod, much better than anything Jimmy Anderson had got out of her. Blair had gone in to see him with the full intention of asking that Hamish Macbeth be kept off the case. Instead, he had been told that Hamish had to be brought into everything.

'I've got someone to interview,' said Hamish, getting into the Land Rover. He drove off, leaving Blair glowering after him.

He stopped on the waterfront when he saw the foxy features of Jimmy Anderson. 'I thought you were going to come and see me,' said Hamish.

'I did, yesterday evening, but there was no one there except that dog of yours up on the kitchen table scoffing something.'

'My dinner,' said Hamish.

'And now he's ripped the boss's trousers. Where are you off to?'

'Tell you later if you come round.'

'Get the whisky ready.'

Hamish drove on to the hotel. The first person he saw when he parked the car was Jerry Darcy, who gave him a cheerful wave. Hamish scowled in reply, and then felt he was being petty. He got down from the Land Rover, meaning to chat to Jerry, but the man was driving off.

Hamish went into the hotel office where the manager, Mr Johnston, was working on the accounts.

'What are you after, Hamish?'

'Mrs Darling.'

'Heather Darling? Don't tell me she's a suspect.'

'No, I just want a wee word with her.'

'She's just about to go off duty. Hang on here for a minute and help yourself to coffee, and I'll fetch her for you.'

Hamish went over to the coffee machine and poured himself a mug of coffee. He had a sudden sharp longing for a cigarette although he had not smoked for some years.

The door opened and Heather Darling walked in, twisting her apron in red, work-roughened hands. She was a small, plump woman with greying hair and a round rosy face.

'Sit down,' said Hamish.

'What's up? Is it Josie?'

'No, nothing's wrong. I just wanted to ask you a few questions about Fergus.'

'The dustman?'

'Yes, him. I believe he was on friendly terms with you and your daughter.'

He knew before she opened her mouth that she was going to repeat word for word what Josie had said. But unlike her daughter, who had a hard streak, Heather Darling was frightened and trying hard not to show it. He wondered whether to use Blair's methods, accuse her of lying and try to break her down. But he had a feeling she would stick to that story through thick and thin. In some way, she was protecting her daughter. To try to put her at her ease, he asked about the wedding.

'It's fine,' said Heather curtly. 'What's it got to do with the murder?'

'Nothing,' said Hamish. 'Look, maybe when you've had time to think you'll remember something.'

Her face set in stubborn lines. Hamish said, 'You know where to find me. I'll be calling on you again.'

'What about?'

'About Fergus's murder. Think about it.' He wondered how Clarry was getting on.

Clarry was at that moment wishing himself anywhere else but in the Currie sisters' cottage, faced by two pairs of baleful eyes behind thick glasses.

'I am just trying to find out if you can remember anything else,' said Clarry.

'And we are wondering,' said Nessie severely, 'what you, an officer of the law, were doing romancing a married woman.'

'A married woman,' muttered the Greek chorus that was her sister.

Clarry turned red. 'I was acting under orders from my superior officer. Martha Macleod was being beaten by her husband. Sergeant Macbeth wanted me to try to get her to make a complaint.'

'And did that mean you should take them out in a boat and turn the police station into a disco?'

'Yes. Kindness towards a family which is in sore need of it may seem strange to you ladies.'

'We are not forgetting our duty,' said Nessie. 'We're going to help her clean up.'

'So now we've got that out of the way,' said Clarry, 'Sergeant Macbeth tells me that you are a very noticing pair of ladies. I would like to ask you if you noticed anything strange the night Fergus was killed.'

'When was he exactly killed, exactly killed?' asked Jessie.

Clarry strove for patience. 'I mean the night you found him in your bin.'

The sisters looked at each other. Then Nessie said, 'It was a quiet evening. That Josie Darling went past . . .'

'At what time?'

'About eight o'clock. Teetering along on a stupid pair of high heels. If I had legs like that I would cover them,' said Nessie, glancing down complacently at her own skinny shanks. 'Before that, it was Mrs Docherty who lives next door. She walked over to the waterfront and looked at the loch. Then she came back. Mrs Wellington, the minister's wife, went by, going to the schoolhouse, I think. She's supervising the arrangements for the new teacher, but that was earlier, about six o'clock.'

'Any strange noises?'

They both shook their heads of rigidly permed hair.

'Well, if you think of anything, let me know.'

Clarry made his way back along the waterfront. He was stopped by Angela Brodie, the doctor's wife. 'Could you give me a bit of help? I and some of the women want to go and help Martha clear out Fergus's things. But we don't want to call too soon and upset her. Do you think you could ask her, you being a friend of hers?'

Clarry's round face brightened at the idea of a legitimate opportunity to go and call on Martha.

'I'll go right away,' he said, touching the peak of his cap.

He swung round and with a light step headed towards Martha's cottage. They were all sitting indoors, the old television flickering in the corner of the living room.

Martha had great dark shadows under her eyes, and she appeared to have lost more weight. Her clothes hung on her thin body.

'Had any supper?' asked Clarry.

'None of us are feeling very hungry.'

'Won't do,' said Clarry. 'You've got to keep your strength up for the children's sake and for your own. Get ready. We're all going down to the Italian restaurant. Dinner's on me.'

Martha saw the way her children brightened up but she hesitated. 'There's the baby.'

'Put the baby in the pram and we'll wheel the pram into the restaurant.'

'Won't they protest, and I'm not properly dressed.'

'It's not the Ritz,' said Clarry. 'Come on.'

Willie Lamont, who used to be Hamish's constable and who now waited table at the restaurant, protested when Martha and Clarry lifted the pram with the sleeping baby into the restaurant.

Clarry took him aside and whispered fiercely, 'They are all in need of a good meal so I won't have any protests from you. That poor woman's been stuck up there in that dingy cottage. The ladies of Lochdubh are going to help her clean up, so if they can help, so can you.'

'Clean up?' Willie's eyes gleamed with an almost religious fervour. 'Nobody can clean like me. Have you tried that new cleaner on the market, Green Lightning? Man, the way it cuts through grease is grand.' And before Clarry could stop him, he headed purposely towards Martha. 'I hear some of the ladies are coming to help you clean. You just say the day, and I'll be there.'

Martha looked at Clarry. 'What's all this about?'

'Angela Brodie and some of the others thought you would feel better if you had a bit of help to clean out your husband's things. But if you'd like to wait a bit . . .'

'No, I don't mind. Any time will do. I'd be glad of the help.'

Mr Ferrari, the owner, joined them. 'Ah, Mrs Macleod,' he said. 'My condolences on your sad loss. You are my guests for this evening. Have anything on the menu you want. Officer Graham, perhaps you would like to see our kitchens?'

Clarry wanted to stay with Martha, but on the other hand, cooking was in his blood. 'Just a wee look,' he said. 'I don't want to leave Mrs Macleod alone for long.'

Clarry was taken on a tour of the kitchens. He had always thought he would be unfit for the restaurant trade, but he could feel his enthusiasm growing. Mr Ferrari crooned in his ear how easy the job of chef would be and how a man interested in food was wasting his time as a police officer.

'You don't know if I can cook,' said Clarry.

'True. Why don't you give it a try on your day off?'

'Maybe I'll do that. Now I'd best get back to Martha and the children.'

Martha, with her wan face and well-behaved children, was creating a good impression among the other customers. In these days of spoilt, whining brats, even the sternest heart melts at the sight of a quiet well-behaved child. People had stopped by the table while Clarry was in the kitchen to give Martha their condolences.

Clarry sat down with them and picked up the menu. He planned to slim down, but a free meal was a free meal. He would diet tomorrow.

They had a simple meal of minestrone, ravioli and huge slices of chocolate cake. Clarry told tales of policing, all highly embroidered, and was pleased to notice that Martha was eating everything.

When he returned to the police station, Hamish was waiting. 'You've been away a long time,' he said.

'It happened like this.' Clarry described how he had ended up in the Italian restaurant.

'You should go carefully,' said Hamish. 'Blair's been round and he's spitting bullets. Seems as if Fergus was killed somewhere else and carried to the bin.' Hamish knew the real reason Blair was furious. He had wanted Hamish off the case and had been told to keep him on.

'So what did you get out of the Currie sisters?'

'Not much,' said Clarry, fumbling for his notebook. 'Do you want me to read out what I've got?'

'Go ahead.'

Clarry read out from his notes. 'See,' he said. 'Nothing there.'

'Yes, there is,' said Hamish Macbeth. 'There's something there that interests me a lot.'

Chapter Four

Ah, make the most of what we yet may spend,
Before we too into the Dust descend;
Dust into Dust, and under Dust, to lie,
Sans Wine, sans Song, sans Singer, and –
   sans End!

— Edward Fitzgerald

Jimmy Anderson poked his head around the kitchen door. 'Come in,' said Hamish. 'Clarry, you'd best go and start typing up your notes, and I'll do mine after.'

When Clarry had left, Hamish asked, 'Well, what's new?'

'What kind of whisky do you have?'

Hamish went to a cupboard and pulled out a bottle of Johnny Walker. 'That'll do fine,' said Jimmy. He waited until Hamish had poured him a generous glassful. Then he said, 'The autopsy report puts the death at about two days before he was found. Didn't those Currie sisters notice the smell before then?'

'Can't have. They only noticed when they lifted the lid.'

'You're slipping, Hamish. Didn't you ask them?'

'I should've. I was too concerned in stopping gossip about Clarry and Martha Macleod.'

Jimmy sipped his whisky and then eyed Hamish speculatively. 'Not like you at all. You're that fat copper's sergeant, not his father. I know he trounced Blair wi' that threat o' the Race Relations Board, but to my mind, he's still a suspect.'

'If he wasnae wi' me, he was with Mrs Macleod.'

'Judging from the contents of the dead man's stomach, he was killed sometime during the night. You don't sleep wi' your copper, do you?'

'It's not him,' said Hamish stubbornly.

'Oh, well, Blair's having a hard time wi' that environment woman. But he's not much interested in this case. He thinks he's got the chance of making a drugs bust. Daviot told him to keep you informed, so he's sulking and saying you can handle it. He's trying to get me put in charge.'

'Can you get me the forensic report?'

'More whisky?'

'Help yourself. The bottle's in front of you.'

'Thanks.' Jimmy poured a large amount into his glass. Then he dug into the inside pocket of his jacket and produced two sheets of paper. 'One copy of a forensic report. Here you are.'

Hamish scanned it. 'Could they judge if he had been killed far from the Curries' bin?'

'No, not far. There was some blood that had leaked from his head into the bin.'

'The Curries live on the waterfront. I cannot believe that in this village, even in the middle of the night, someone carried a dead body and put it in that bin, without a soul seeing anything. Wait a bit. The bin's round the side. The lane to Martha's runs up the side of the cottage. And it's a low fence. Did they find anything there?'

'They're still working on it. But, say, two people could have done it. One to lift the body over the fence, another to catch it and put it in the bin.'

'But why the Curries?'

'I spoke to Nessie Currie. She seemed proud of the fact that she was the greenest person in Lochdubh, and Fergus didn't appreciate it. Food refuse goes into the compost heap apart from the stuff they give to Mrs Docherty next door for her hens. Jessie says they have the least rubbish of anyone in Lochdubh. So whoever did it would guess the body wouldn't be found for some time.'

'Ah, that's daft. Anyone who didn't want the body found could've weighted it down and dumped it in the loch. Or taken it up on the moors and sunk it into a peat bog. No, putting

Fergus in a dustbin has an element of revenge and hatred in it, even after the man was killed. To tell the truth, I don't know a soul in Lochdubh with that sort of character, or motivation. There is one odd thing. There's a wee lassie up the back of the harbour, name of Josie Darling; getting married in two weeks' time. Now she goes on as if she's a glamour puss, but she's just a wee village girl. But she was friendly with Fergus. And she's hiding something. I'm going to have another go at her tomorrow.'

'Aye, well, you'd better concentrate a bit more. Forget about Clarry.'

They talked for some time, going over and over the case. Clarry came in. 'Typed up my notes, sir. What about lunch?'

'That would be grand,' said Jimmy before Hamish could reply.

'I've nothing much in the house,' said Clarry, easing round them to the stove. 'But I could make a cheese omelette.'

Jimmy drank, and he watched, amused as Clarry deftly whipped eggs. Soon he was placing three plates of fluffy omelette in front of them.

'Great,' said Jimmy. 'You pair ought to get married.' He saw Lugs put a paw on Hamish's knee. 'Does your dog eat cheese omelette?'

'I've got something for him.' Clarry took down a bowl of chopped liver he had cooked earlier from a rack above the cooker and placed it on the floor.

'That's an odd-looking dog,' said Jimmy. 'But any dog that can attack Blair and tear his trousers deserves the best food.'

After Jimmy had left, Hamish said to Clarry, 'Check at that new hotel if there are any workers apart from the locals. I've got a call to make. Come on, Lugs. Walk.'

With the dog trotting along beside him he walked to Mrs Docherty's cottage. He tied the leash to the fence and then knocked at the door.

Mrs Docherty was a tired-looking middle-aged woman with grey hair and small eyes. When she answered the door and saw Hamish standing there, a closed look came over her face, and she said primly, 'What is it?'

'I wanted a word with you.'

'What about?'

'About the murder.'

'It's got nothing to do with me.'

'I chust wanted to ask you a few questions. Is your man at home?'

'No, he's working in Strathbane.'

'Can I come in?'

'No, I'm cleaning.'

'Then we'll talk in the garden. I want to ask you if you saw or heard anything. Fergus's body was put in the bin soon after he was murdered.'

'I didn't see or hear anything. Why ask me?'

Hamish remembered Clarry telling him that the Curries had seen Mrs Docherty walk across the road and stare at the loch and walk back again. It was just a small thing, and yet, Mrs Docherty, like the rest of the locals, was so used to the magnificent scenery around her that she barely noticed. He'd had a mental picture of a worried woman going out to stare blindly at the loch. But maybe his imagination had run away with him.

'I heard that on the evening Fergus was found, you went out of your cottage and walked across and looked at the loch, and then walked back again.'

'So what's wrong with that?'

'It struck me as the action of someone who was deeply worried about something.'

'Havers,' she said briskly. 'I often go and have a look at the loch.'

'Why?'

'Why? Do I need a reason? Because it's there.'

She was afraid of something, of that Hamish was sure, and it couldn't be because she was being interviewed by a policeman. No one in Lochdubh was afraid of him.

'I'll be back,' he said. He walked out of the small garden and unhitched Lugs and walked away. Mrs Docherty stood watching his tall figure and clenched and unclenched her hands.

Hamish went back to the station and typed up his notes and then faxed the little he had, along with Clarry's notes, to Strathbane.

Clarry came in just as he finished. 'Anything?' asked Hamish.

'Apart from the secretary, a Miss Stathos, the rest are locals. Miss Stathos says Mr Ionides plans to hire local staff as well when he's ready to open, waiters and maids and manager and all that.'

Hamish leaned back in his chair. 'Oh, my, that means he'll go after the staff at the Tommel Castle Hotel.'

'Maybe they'll stay loyal.'

'Times are hard. If he offers higher wages, then they'll go.'

'There don't seem to be any reporters left.'

'There's a triple murder in Inverness. They'll rely on the local man from now on. At least we should get a bit o' peace.'

Four more days went by, during which Jimmy Anderson, Hamish and Clarry assiduously interviewed the population of Lochdubh. Hamish went over forensic reports. The ground at the lane beside the Currie sisters' garden had been hard with all the dry weather and had not yielded anything. The side of the house and at the back where the bin stood was covered in gravel.

Frustrated, Hamish decided to examine the place closely for himself. He realized that like everyone else these days, he had been blinded by the glories of forensic science and had assumed they had missed nothing.

He knew the Currie sisters had gone up to Martha's cottage with Mrs Wellington and Angela to clear out Fergus's things.

He carried a large magnifying glass, and, feeling ridiculous, feeling that he looked like a stage detective, he began to go over every inch of ground along with the fence and the road at the side. The rain he had expected had not yet arrived although the air was moist and damp.

After two hours, he was about to give up, when he saw a little spark of colour between the fence posts. He took out a pair of tweezers and eased out a tiny little pink thread of material. It was so small that when he took the magnifying glass away from his eye, he could barely see it. He put it in a plastic envelope. He would wait until the Curries had finished cleaning and ask them if they had any idea where it might have come from.

Angela was glad she had given the children some money for sweets and had sent them off, for Mrs Wellington was trying to persuade Martha that some of Fergus's clothes could be cut down for the boys.

Surprisingly it was Nessie who stood up to the domineering minister's wife. 'Leave her be,' said Nessie firmly. 'She doesn't want anything of her man left in the cottage.'

'Left in the cottage,' echoed Jessie, and both sisters glared at Mrs Wellington.

'Well, let's bag up the stuff, and I'll take it into a charity shop in Strathbane,' said Mrs Wellington, capitulating.

The women worked busily, bagging up suits and shirts, socks and underwear. Martha, finding Angela the most sympathetic, kept close to her. In the bedroom Martha had shared with Fergus, Angela said, 'The rugs in here could do with throwing out. I've got a nice carpet in the loft at home. My husband didn't like it because it's bright red, but it's warm and cheery. Where did you get these rugs?'

'They're awful, aren't they?' said Martha with a weak smile. 'Fergus found them in someone's rubbish at a croft house and brought them home. They're all cigarette burns.'

'I'll take them away and bring you the carpet,' said Angela. 'No, please take it. It's a waste of a good carpet if it stays in my loft. Let's just roll up these dreadful rugs.'

Angela got down on her knees and started to roll up one by the window. 'There's a floorboard been sawn here,' she said. 'Is this where you hide the family jewels?'

Martha walked over and stared down. One of the floorboards had been sawn to make a square like a lid. 'I never really noticed that before,' she said. 'I'm sorry the floor's dirty. I was going to wash it, but Fergus shouted at me to leave it alone.'

'Mind if I have a look and see if there's anything down there?' asked Angela.

'No, go ahead.'

'I need something to lift it, a screwdriver or something.'

'I'll get one. There's a toolbox under the bed.'

Martha came back after a few moments with a screwdriver. Angela prised up the sawn square of wood. She peered in the cavity. Then she reached down and pulled out a plastic envelope with what appeared to be several letters in it. Angela peered through the plastic. Some of the letters seemed to be covered in food stains and coffee stains.

'I think if you don't mind, Martha, I'll just take this along to Hamish Macbeth. I would let you look at it first, but it might be important, and I don't want to get too many fingerprints on it.'

'Go ahead,' said Martha wearily.

Angela hurried out and made her way to the police station. A light rain was beginning to fall. Oh well, thought Angela sadly, it's not often we've had a summer like this one. It couldn't last forever.

She saw the tall figure of Hamish in front of her and hurried to catch up with him.

'Hamish,' she said. 'Look what I found under the floorboards in Fergus's bedroom.'

He took the plastic envelope from her. 'It seems to be letters, Hamish. There might be a clue.'

'Thanks, Angela. I'll take it into the station and have a look at it.'

'I'd better get back before Mrs Wellington bullies poor Martha to death!'

Hamish hurried into the police station, into the office, sat down at his desk and gingerly eased the letters out with the tweezers he had used earlier.

The first one had been written to Josie Darling. He read: 'Dear Josie, I just can't go through with it. I'm sorry to let you down at the last minute, but I've met someone else, and it's real love this time. If you need any help writing apology letters or returning the presents, let me know. You'll hate me for a bit, but after time passes, you'll come to realize I did the right thing. I hope you, too, will find someone. Yours, aye, Murdo.'

'The bastard!' said Hamish out loud. Lugs scrabbled at his knee. 'Down, boy,' said Hamish sharply. He put the letter carefully to one side. Then he picked up the next. 'Dear Helen, I'll never forget our night in Strathbane. I'm still travelling around but I hope to be back in Strathbane soon. Any chance of you getting away from your old man? Give us a bell if you can, snookums. Always your loving Pat.'

Who was Helen? wondered Hamish. The next was a letter to crofter Angus Ettrik. It was from his bank manager. Hamish scanned it rapidly. It was telling Angus that he could have no further credit.

The fourth was an old newspaper cutting. It read: 'Mrs Fiona McClellan appeared at Strathbane sheriff's court yesterday charged with shoplifting. A psychiatrist, Dr J. Arthur, testified that Mrs McClellan was now undergoing treatment for kleptomania. Sheriff Paul Tampley gave Mrs McClellan a suspended sentence of one year but told her that should she appear in his court again, then he would not be so lenient.'

Hamish's heart sank lower. Mrs McClellan was the bank manager's wife.

There could only be one explanation as to why Fergus had kept these items hidden under the floorboards. Blackmail.

Hamish groaned and put his head in his hands. He should phone Strathbane immediately and reveal the contents of what Angela had found. Blair would descend like the wrath of God. He was a great man for arresting first and asking questions afterwards. Four lives might be needlessly ruined.

He looked down at his dog, who stared back up at him with those-odd blue eyes. 'I'll give it a day, Lugs. One day. Let's see what they have to say for themselves. But who's Helen?'

* * *

'Did your husband know?'

'No, I was terrified of him finding out. He was manager of the main bank in Strathbane when I was charged. He felt ashamed of me. He moved us here. I got treatment, and I haven't lapsed since. I knew my husband couldn't bear Lochdubh knowing about my past. He would have moved again, and this time, I don't think he would have taken me with him.'

'How much did Fergus want?'

'One thousand pounds. I told him I couldn't get that much together without my husband finding out so he said he would take it in installments. I had paid him two hundred by the time he was murdered. Now it's all for nothing. You're here and there is nothing to stop the misery happening all over again.'

'What were you doing on the night of July twenty-second?'

'I was chairing the Mother's Union at the church. Then I came home and watched a bit of television with my husband. Then we both went to bed. Will you be taking me to Strathbane?'

'As to that,' said Hamish, 'I will try to keep this quiet, for the moment. But I want you to let me know if you hear anything, however small, that might relate to the case.'

She looked at him, her eyes suddenly full of hope. 'Are you saying you might be able to keep this quiet?'

'I'll do my best for a few days.'

'But if you don't find the murderer, then this will all have to come out?'

'I'm afraid so.'

'Then I will do my very best to find something out for you. Thank you.'

Hamish, going towards Martha's cottage, met Angela on her way home. 'Did you tell the Currie sisters or Mrs Wellington about the letters?' asked Hamish.

'No, and I don't think Martha said anything either.'

'Angela, that wee scunner Fergus was using information he found in the rubbish to blackmail a few people. I'll need to let Strathbane know eventually. But if I can protect them for a few days, I will. I'll speak to Martha. Get her to say she just found them when I tell her to.'

'That's awful, Hamish. Fergus deserved to be murdered.'

'Nobody deserves to be murdered.'

'He did,' said Angela firmly.

Hamish was turning away when he turned back and asked, 'Can you think of any Helens in the village?'

'Helen? Let me see, there's Helen Macgregor out on the Braikie side, there's Helen Jensen, but she's just a wee schoolgirl, there's Helen Docherty . . .'

'Mrs Docherty? Her name's Helen?'

'Yes.'

'Right.' Hamish strode off and left Angela staring after him.

Martha opened the door to him and invited him inside. The cottage had a polished and scrubbed look. 'I only wanted them to take away Fergus's things,' said Martha, 'but they insisted on doing the housekeeping as well. Was there anything in those letters that Angela found?'

'That's what I want to talk to you about. Have you looked at your husband's bankbook?'

'No, not yet.'

'Did he leave a will?'

'He did. He left everything to me, such as it is.'

'Good. Right. Here's the problem. It is my belief your husband was a blackmailer.'

'Oh, no!' Martha wailed.

'He was using letters he found in the rubbish. I'm keeping it quiet at the moment, Martha. It's all right if I call you Martha?'

'Yes.'

'We're Hamish and Martha unless we're being official. Now let's see that bankbook.'

'It's in a drawer in the sideboard.' Martha went to the sideboard which was one of those awful cheap thirties pieces of furniture made of yellowish wood and badly carved. She jerked one of the doors open and produced a Bank of Scotland bankbook.

Hamish studied it. There was the payment of two hundred, probably from Mrs Mc-Clellan, then there was another payment of five hundred pounds, and everything else was Fergus's salary.

'I may ask you to pay back the money he extorted from people, Martha. But I can't do anything until I find the murderer. You see, the thing is, if I take the letters to the police, a lot of innocent villagers might suffer, get their reputations ruined. I must ask you not to talk about this.'

'I wouldn't dream of it,' gasped Martha. 'Oh, the shame of it!' She suddenly turned a muddy colour. 'But Hamish, what if one of them he was blackmailing killed him, and they think I've got the proof?'

'I've thought of that, believe me. Whoever did it will know your cottage has been searched from top to bottom. You were searched, weren't you?'

She nodded dumbly.

'How they missed that bit in the bedroom floor is beyond me.'

'They weren't looking for anything like that,' said Martha. 'I mean, I showed them the will, the bankbook, but there was nothing else in that drawer, and they seemed satisfied with that. They were talking about some football match back in Strathbane and wondering if they could wrap things up and get back in time.'

Hamish reflected that people only read in their newspapers about murderers being caught by one hair or saliva on a cigarette and never heard about the ones where the investigating team wanted to get back in time for a football match and possibly missed something important. If Martha had killed her husband, whatever clues might have been left had been scrubbed away by the helpful ladies of Lochdubh.

'I'll let you know how I get on,' he said. 'But I can only keep this quiet for a few days.'

He was heading for the door when Martha asked, 'How's Clarry?'

'He's fine.'

'Give him my regards.'

'Will do.' Hamish walked out. He had a sudden awful thought that a battered wife like Martha might have seen in Clarry the husband she had always wanted and had hammered her husband to death. He shook his head to clear it. He'd better interview the other suspects fast and trust to his instinct.

He walked down to Mrs Docherty's cottage and knocked on the door. Her husband, he remembered, worked at the fish counter in a supermarket in Strathbane. Mrs Docherty opened the door. Her eyes dilated with fright, and then she masked it with fury. 'This is police harassment.'

'You must have been expecting me to call for some time. How long was Fergus Macleod blackmailing you?'

She stood very still. Then she said wearily, 'You'd better come in.'

She led the way into a tidy little living room. 'I prayed he would have got rid of that letter. I knew the police had searched his cottage. When I didn't hear anything, I thought I was safe. Will I be arrested?'

'Not yet,' said Hamish. 'I'm still trying to keep it quiet for a few days. But if I don't find the murderer in that time, I'll need to go to Strathbane. What happened?'

'I'm fifty-five.'

'I don't see what . . .'

'Listen. Us women up in the Highlands don't reach the menopause until fifty-seven. Sometimes the scientists say it's the fresh fish and others say it's the whisky. Anyway, I knew I hadn't long. To be a real woman, that is. I was in Strathbane, shopping, and I decided to go to the bar of the Royal Hotel for a drink. That's where I met Pat. You're not taking notes.'

'Not yet,' said Hamish. 'Just let's hope it won't be necessary.'

'Anyway, we got talking. I drank a bit too much. He made me laugh. Then he suggested I come back that evening to spend the night with him. Just like that. I said, why not? I didn't really mean to keep that date. I mean, I knew I was a bit drunk and shouldn't even be driving. When I got home, Roger phoned.'

'Your husband?'

'Yes. He said he was going to the Rotary Club. He said he would be staying the night with a friend of ours. I must have been mad. I decided to go for it. It wasn't worth it. I felt miserable and ashamed in the morning. Just to get away nicely, like a fool I gave him my address. When I got that letter, I didn't put it in one of the paper boxes, I put it in with the general rubbish. But that ferret of a man was sifting through everyone's rubbish.'

'Why now?' said Hamish. 'I mean, why did he suddenly start blackmailing? I mean, if that letter had been in the box for papers, I could understand it. I could understand him being tempted. But to suddenly take it out of the general rubbish. Maybe he'd already stumbled on to something profitable.'

'I'm not the only one?'

'No. Where were you the night Fergus was murdered?'

'I went out to a meeting at the church, came home, watched a bit of television with my husband and went to bed. Oh, please, can you try to stop this getting out?'

'I'll do my best. Let me know if you hear anything. Anything at all.'

'I must have been mad,' she said, half to herself. 'I've always been respectable. The boys are doing well, both in jobs in Glasgow. I blame the television.'

'How's that?'

'Well, women like me sit up here in the very north of Scotland, night after night, watching beautiful people. Morals never seem to bother them. Then the day comes when women like me think, I'll have some of that. And some of that turns out to be a sordid night with a travelling salesman. Men sleep around, why shouldn't women? That's what they preach on the box. But to old-fashioned women like me, I can't get rid of the old values of loyalty and modesty. Do you remember when modesty in women was considered a virtue?'

'I'm not old enough,' said Hamish ruefully.

After he had left Mrs Docherty, he went back to the police station. Jimmy Anderson was sitting in the police office, his feet on the desk.

'Where's Clarry?' asked Hamish.

'I sent him off on a tour of the village, asking as many people as possible if they saw anything. I've got two coppers from Strathbane doing the same thing. Get anything?'

'Not much,' said Hamish.

'That's not like you. Come on. You've got something up your sleeve.'

'Not me. I'm off to check some of the outlying crofts. What are you going to do?'

'Coordinate,' said Jimmy vaguely. 'Take that weird dog of yours with you. I thought he wasn't going to let me into the station.'

'So how'd you get in?'

'One whole packet of chocolate wafer biscuits.'

'Whit? You're a bad man, Jimmy. You'll ruin his teeth.'

Hamish went into the bathroom and collected his toothbrush and toothpaste. Then he grabbed the unsuspecting Lugs from under the kitchen table and began to forcibly brush the dog's teeth. Then he put the dog down in front of his water bowl. He drank thirstily and then looked accusingly up at Hamish.

'Come on, boy. It's no use you looking at me like that. How can you bite Blair if your teeth fall out?'

Soon Hamish was driving off out of Lochdubh with a sulky Lugs on the seat beside him.

Angus Ettrik's croft lay off the Drim road. He turned up a narrow lane, stopping at one point to get down and shoo some of Angus's sheep back into the fields.

Angus's wife, Kirsty, was hanging out sheets in the garden, although it was not really a garden, more a dump for old machinery. A washing machine leaned against a television set. Two rusting cars and various bits of machinery stood testament to the Highland crofter's weakness. Nothing was ever thrown away because it 'might come in handy sometime'.

'What's up?' asked Kirsty, coming towards him. She was a small, dark, gypsy-looking woman.

'Angus about?'

'He's up at the peats. What's it about?'

'Just asking everyone round about.'

'Oh, the murder. That was awful, so it was.'

Hamish nodded to her and got into the Land Rover and then drove as far as he could along a heathery track.

He finally got down and, followed by Lugs, walked the last half mile to the peat stacks. Angus was cutting peats. As Hamish approached him, he turned over in his mind what he knew about the crofter. He had a reputation of being lazy, but that wasn't unusual in the Highlands where the doctor's surgery was at its busiest on a Monday morning with men complaining of bad backs. He and Kirsty did not have children. He was a small wiry man with a thick shock of dark hair going grey at the sides. His face was permanently tanned from working outdoors.

He saw Hamish but continued to cut peats. He had a tractor and trailer beside him. The trailer was already loaded up with cut peats, like dark slices of cake.

'How's it going, Angus?'

Angus paused and looked up at the tall policeman. 'What do ye want?'

'I want to know if Fergus Macleod was blackmailing you.'

Angus looked down. 'Havers,' he muttered. Then he raised his head. 'Do I look like the sort o' cheil that would let a dustman blackmail me?'

'He had found a letter from your bank refusing to let you have any more credit.'

'And do you think he would try to blackmail a poor crofter wi' that? Man, you know the situation in the Highlands. It's crawlin' these days wi' crofters getting letters like that. But I haff my pride, and I don't want them at Strathbane pawing over letters to me!'

'I can't suppress evidence – well, not for much longer, Angus. It's probably of no importance and yet, why did he keep it? Did he call on you?'

'Chust to empty the bins, him and his silly uniform.'

'We'll leave it for the moment. I still can't figure out why Fergus would keep such a letter unless he hoped to get something out of it.'

'That's your job, isn't it?' sneered Angus. 'Always looking for dirt. Well, good clean peat dirt iss all you'll be finding here.'

'Think about it,' said Hamish. 'Where were you the night Fergus was killed?'

'What night would that be?'

'July twenty-second.'

'I wass down on the waterfront having a jar wi' some o' the fishermen afore they went out.'

'The bar's closed.'

'Aye, but we wass just sitting on the harbour wall, Archie Maclean, me and the others, having a smoke and a crack.'

'I'll check that. Then what?'

'Then I walked home. I didnae want to drive so I hadnae the car.'

'And you didn't see Fergus on that night?'

'Not a sight.'

'Right. But think again why he might have kept that letter.'

Angus bent to cutting peats and Hamish walked away, followed by his dog. When he got to the Land Rover, he drove back to Angus's croft and called in at the kitchen door. 'Anybody home?'

Kirsty appeared, wiping her hands on her apron. 'I've just been to see your man, Kirsty. I found a letter from your bank manager among Fergus's effects, and I wondered if he had been trying to blackmail you.'

She looked shocked. 'I neffer heard the like. Why blackmail us? That letter should've told him we didn't have any money.'

'That's what puzzles me,' said Hamish.

'He wass friendly enough,' said Kirsty. 'We neffer had any trouble wi' him taking our rubbish, not like them in Lochdubh.' Her eyes fell to Lugs, and she gave a little shriek.

'What's up?' asked Hamish.

'That dog of yours. You shouldnae hae a dog like that.'

'Why?'

'It's got blue eyes.'

'So?'

Kirsty lowered her voice. 'Animals wi' eyes like that are people who've come back. Get it out of here. It's bad luck.'

Lugs suddenly darted round Hamish and into the cottage. Kirsty let out a wail of terror and threw her apron over her head. 'Get it out!' she screamed.

Hamish pushed past her into the kitchen and scooped up his dog, who was sitting under the stove, looking longingly up at a stew pot which was simmering on the hob.

Tucking the dog firmly under one arm, he marched out of the cottage. Kirsty was sitting on a rock, keening and holding her arms tightly about her body.

'Come on, Kirsty,' said Hamish. 'It iss chust the wee dog.'

'Go away,' whispered Kirsty.

Hamish shrugged helplessly. Although he suffered from a fair amount of Highland superstition himself, he was still amazed at how extreme it could be in other Highlanders.

He carried Lugs back to the Land Rover. Better check with Archie whether Angus had been where he said he had been on the night Fergus had been killed.

'Aye, I mind fine he was here,' said Archie, sitting like a gnome on the harbour wall in the tight suit he usually sported and which the villagers swore his wife boiled, dried and ironed.

'At what time?'

'Early-ish. About seven o'clock. We was just about to go out, but Niven had a bottle o' whisky and we passed it around.'

'So what was Angus talking about?'

'Price o' sheep. Usual crofter's complaint.'

'Did he talk about Fergus?'

'Wait a bit. We was saying what a wee bastard the dustman was and Angus said something like, he was all right if you got on the right side of him.'

'Anything else?'

'No, then we had to go out to the fishing. He said he would walk home. I said, that's a fair walk, and he said he was used to it and with petrol prices going up, we'd all have to learn to walk like in the old days. He left about seven o'clock.'

'They think from the contents of the stomach that Fergus was killed some time later that evening. Someone must have heard something. This is a village. Someone must have been looking out.'

'Inspector Morse was on television. That waud be from eight o'clock to ten.'

'The whole o' Lochdubh can't have been watching Inspector Morse.'

'If my ain wife wouldnae miss it, then no one else is going to.'

Momentarily amused by the fact that the Highland villagers should find murder and mayhem in the Oxford colleges so enthralling, Hamish then said, 'So you got the impression that Fergus was friendly with Angus?'

'I couldnae say for sure. But he was the only

one of us not to have a hard word to say for Fergus.'

'And how's Callum McSween coping?'

'He's different. He's such a cheery man that we thought, well why not put the damn things in the right bins. If Fergus had been like him, we'd all have gone along with it.'

Hamish walked back to the police station. Clarry was out. Hamish hoped he was working and not wandering around the shelves of Patel's store, planning elaborate meals. He fed Lugs and sat down in the police office, turning over and over the little he knew. If nothing broke, then he was going to be obliged to turn the letters over to Blair. Then he suddenly thought of Mrs Fleming. To interfere at such cost in the sanitation of a small Highland village surely betrayed some fanaticism. He looked up as Jimmy Anderson strolled in.

'No Blair?' asked Hamish.

'No, and my feet are sore. It's a small village. I decided to go round everyone myself, but your man, Clarry, always seemed to have been there just before me.'

'What about Mrs Fleming?'

'That tart? What about her?'

'I keep wondering what's behind all this greening o' Lochdubh.'

Jimmy grinned. 'I know, you think she thought Fergus wasn't doing his job so she hit him with the hammer.'

'Sounds daft. But what do we know of her?'

'She was just an ordinary councillor. Then suddenly she gets promoted to Director of the Environment. Rumour has it the provost got into her knickers.'

'My, my. I might have a word wi' her if it's not interfering with your investigations.'

'Interfere all you like. I'm needed back in Strathbane. Let me know what you get.'

Hamish left a note on the kitchen table for Clarry to walk his dog and then got into the Land Rover. He slowed to a crawl as he passed the schoolhouse. A beautiful vision was standing by a removal van supervising the arrival of furniture. Her lovely features were surrounded by a cloud of black hair. Her eyes were large and blue. She had a perfect figure and long, long legs. Hamish grinned. The new schoolteacher had arrived. If he got back early enough, he would invite her out to dinner and hope that word would get back to Priscilla.

In Strathbane, he learned that Mrs Fleming was too busy to see him for another hour. He passed the time wandering about, looking at the shops. He was heading back to the council offices when he suddenly saw Priscilla. She was looking in a jeweller's window with Jerry. Hamish's heart plummeted. Were they choosing a ring? He walked away quickly before they could see him. Then he glanced at his watch. Time to visit the formidable Mrs Fleming.

'Sit down, Officer,' was her cold greeting. She eyed the tall, lanky sergeant with disfavour. 'I have already spoken at length to your superiors from headquarters. What do you want?'

Hamish sat down opposite her and put his peaked cap on the desk. 'I am examining all points of this case. To go back to the beginning, why did you choose Lochdubh for this greening experiment when Strathbane is more in need of it?'

'I am *passionate* about the environment. Strathbane is a massive project. I wanted to start the experiment with somewhere smaller. Somewhere that would look good on the television cameras.'

'Television?'

'Yes, *don't you see*? It pays to *advertise*. Lochdubh is a picturesque village. When it appears on the screens, people in the Highlands will feel *compelled* to follow the good example.'

'They may have more important news to cover than the cleaning up of a Highland village,' said Hamish maliciously. 'Like the odd war or two.'

'I thought of that,' she said, leaning forward. 'We are now in August, and August is traditionally a quiet time for news. I have the press handouts ready. I will be arriving in Lochdubh with the councillors and provost, and I will make a speech to the cameras.'

Her eyes took on a dreamy, faraway look. Oh my, thought Hamish, a star is born.

'Fergus Macleod was not popular,' said Hamish. 'In fact, he was so unpopular that the villagers were not putting their rubbish in the correct receptacles. They are now.'

Her eyes became steely. 'Are you daring to suggest that I might have murdered some dustman because the project was not working out?'

'Of course not,' said Hamish quickly. 'I'm just asking questions here and there and trying to build up a picture.'

'Then may I suggest you get back to your village where the murder took place and get on with your job in the right location? The murderer must be found. Fergus Macleod was as dedicated to the environment as I am myself.'

Hamish eyed her curiously. 'If I may say so, Mrs Fleming, it is my humble opinion that you would look well on television.'

She cast her eyes down in false modesty. Then she said, 'Whether I look good or not, that is beside the point. I wish to do my best for the environment.'

Liar, thought Hamish. He stood up. 'When is this ceremony to be?'

'Next week, on Wednesday. I hope the weather will be fine. Perhaps you could ask the fishermen to deck their boats with flags? And perhaps it might be in order to give me some sort of presentation from the grateful villagers. Just a large box. There doesn't need to be anything in it. Just for the cameras. And perhaps a pretty wee lassie to give me some flowers.'

Hamish nodded and left. What a monumental ego, he thought with wonder. But would she kill just to get her face on the telly? Television seemed to affect people like a drug. Look at the *Jerry Springer Show*. How could people humiliate themselves in such a way, and all to get their faces in front of the cameras.

He realized he had not asked her where she was on the night Fergus was killed. He half turned and then turned back. She would rant and rave that he was accusing her and report him to Blair. He nodded to Mrs Fleming's secretary, who was sitting at a desk in an adjoining room. She was a small neat girl with a white face, small eyes and large red mouth.

Hamish paused in front of her desk and decided to take a gamble. 'Must be awful, a pretty lass like you, working for that old dragon,' he said.

She let out a scared little giggle. 'Shh, she'll hear you!'

Hamish leaned over the desk. 'Would you be free for a drink this evening?'

'Maybe.'

111

'When do you finish?'

'Five o'clock.'

'What about then?'

She giggled again. 'Oh, all right.'

'I'll see you in the cocktail bar of the Grand just after five.'

The phone on her desk rang. 'All right,' she said again.

Hamish went off. It would be interesting to quiz the secretary and find out more about Mrs Fleming.

Chapter Five

Dear, beauteous death, the jewel of the just!
Shining nowhere but in the dark;
What mysteries do lie beyond thy dust,
Could man outlook that mark!
— Henry Vaughan

Hamish took out his mobile phone and called Jimmy Anderson. 'I just wondered,' said Hamish, 'whether you had ever managed to trace that phone call? You know, the one Fergus got before he went out?'

'Oh, that,' said Jimmy. 'Useless. Came from that phone box on the waterfront.'

'Get Clarry to ask if anybody saw anyone in the box. A light comes on at night.'

'Aye, but it was still light at the time he got the call. What are you up to?'

'Just doing a few inquiries about Mrs Fleming.'

'Waste of time,' said Jimmy. 'I'll get Clarry to ask around and see if anybody saw anyone phoning.'

Hamish rang off and then on impulse dialled the minister's wife. 'I saw the new schoolteacher arrive,' he said.

'So?' barked Mrs Wellington. Hamish began to curse himself for phoning her. He should have tried Angela instead.

'I thought maybe I should take her out for dinner, it being her first night.'

'What a good idea!' exclaimed Mrs Wellington, much to Hamish's surprise.

'I have the schoolhouse number, but what is her name?'

'Mrs Moira Cartwright. A divorcée.'

Hamish thanked her. After he had said goodbye, he wondered how he had got information about the new schoolteacher so easily from Mrs Wellington. It would have been more her style to caution him against romancing the new teacher. He phoned the schoolhouse and a brisk voice answered the phone. 'Mrs Cartwright?'

'Yes, who is this?'

'This is Sergeant Hamish Macbeth. I heard you had just moved in. You must be too busy to make a meal this evening. I wondered whether you would like to meet me for dinner at, say, eight o'clock at the Italian restaurant?'

'Is that the place on the waterfront?'

'The same.'

'That's very kind of you. I'll be there. Good-bye.'

Hamish beamed as he tucked his mobile phone back in his pocket. Forget Priscilla. Or maybe, just maybe, Priscilla might see him with such a beauty.

He then made his way to the Grand Hotel and went into the cocktail bar to wait for Mrs Fleming's secretary.

Clarry was moving patiently from house to house, particularly those near the phone box. No one so far had seen anything. He was walking back along the waterfront when he saw the Macleod children coming towards him.

'How's your mother?' he asked Johnny.

'She's trying to get rid o' that man from the restaurant,' said Johnny. 'She telt him the house was clean, but he's cleaning everything again.'

'I'll see to it,' said Clarry. 'Come with me.'

From Hamish, Clarry had heard tales of Willie Lamont's fanatical cleaning. Followed by the children, he marched up to Martha's cottage.

Martha was sitting on a chair outside the front door. From inside came the frantic sound of scrubbing.

'I can't seem to stop him,' said Martha helplessly.

'I'll stop him. When's the funeral?'

'They're going to release the body next

115

week, they say. If only you could find out who did it. I'll never be at peace until then.'

'I'll find out,' said Clarry stoutly. He went in to confront Willie.

'Get out of here!' roared Clarry. 'And stop persecuting a poor widow woman!'

Willie, who was down on his hands and knees with a scrubbing brush, turned a pained face up to Clarry. 'I was just doing my bit for the community.'

'Well, do it somewhere else. Out!'

'Weellie!' called a voice from outside.

Willie leapt to his feet. 'The wife!' He went outside and Clarry followed him. Clarry had not met Willie's wife before, and he blinked at the vision of Italian loveliness facing him.

'Weellie,' said Lucia Lamont severely. 'You are wanted in the restaurant.'

'Right,' said Willie meekly.

Lucia gave Martha a dazzling smile. 'You must not mind him. He loves cleaning.'

The odd couple walked off arm in arm.

'Come inside,' said Martha to Clarry. 'I'll make us some tea.'

Clarry happily went with her into the cottage, followed by the children. Johnny came in carrying the baby, which he put on Clarry's lap. 'So how are you all bearing up?' asked Clarry.

'We're still in shock,' said Martha.

'What you all need,' said Clarry predictably, 'is a good feed and a funny video.'

'Oh, Clarry,' said Martha, and she began to cry.

Clarry handed the baby to Johnny and went and clumsily patted Martha's shoulder. 'Don't cry. Clarry's here. I'll look after you all.'

Johnny grabbed his arm and looked up into his face.

'Forever?' he asked.

'If your mother would like that,' said Clarry, feeling bolder now, gathering Martha into his arms.

Hamish left the Grand Hotel feeling flat. He had elicited nothing much from the secretary that he did not know already – that since the death of her husband, Mrs Fleming had gone power mad. But whether her craving for power and fame would drive her to killing one dustman seemed too far-fetched.

Then he brightened. There was dinner with the new schoolteacher to look forward to. Just time to get back and change.

Clarry was not there. Hamish let Lugs out into the garden at the back and then prepared some food for the dog. He had a quick bath and shave and then was brushing his teeth when he realized with horror that he had forgotten to buy a new toothbrush. He was brushing his teeth with the brush he had used on Lugs. He shuddered and rinsed out his mouth.

When he let Lugs in, the dog glanced up at him and, as if registering the glory of suit, collar and tie, crept to his food bowl with his tail between his legs. Hamish dressed for the evening meant no company for Lugs.

Hamish found he was excited with anticipation. He remembered the glorious beauty of the vision he had seen beside the removal truck. All thoughts of the murder of Fergus, all speculation about who had murdered Fergus, had gone from his head. Although the nights were drawing in, it was still light and the flanks of the two mountains which soared above the village were bright with heather. One early star shone in the clear, pale greenish-blue of the evening sky, and the setting sun sent a fiery path across the black waters of the loch. The air was full of the smells of a Highland village: tar and peat smoke, strong tea, pine and the salt tang of the waters of the sea loch.

He straightened his tie and went into the restaurant. There were various customers, some he recognized and some he did not. People came from far and wide to dine at the restaurant.

Willie appeared at his elbow. 'I've put her at your usual table, over by the window.'

Hamish looked across. A squat middle-aged woman was sitting there. She had a greyish heavy face with a great wide mouth. Her large pale eyes had thick, fleshy lids. Her salt and pepper hair was secured at her neck with a black velvet bow. She looked like an eighteenth-century man from a Hogarth engraving.

'There's some mistake,' hissed Hamish. 'I'm meeting the new schoolteacher.'

'Well, that's her.'

'You sure?'

'Introduced herself,' said Willie. 'Said she was meeting you.'

The sun disappeared outside the restaurant windows and the sun set in Hamish's heart. He cautiously approached the table.

'Mrs Cartwright?'

She grinned up at him, exposing yellowing and irregular teeth. 'Mr Macbeth, how kind of you to entertain me on my first night.'

Hamish sat down opposite her. 'We're a friendly village. What would you like to drink?'

'Campari and soda, please.'

'So I gather you've just arrived,' said Hamish. 'I saw the removal van. Come from far?'

'From Edinburgh. I hate moving. But I have a super efficient niece, Flora. You fuss too much, Auntie, she said. Let me organize the whole thing.'

'You should have brought her with you,' said Hamish.

'Oh, she went straight back to Edinburgh. She's an advocate, and she's got a case coming up tomorrow.'

There was a silence while they studied the menu. When she had selected what she wanted, Hamish gave their order.

He thought of Priscilla and felt a weight of unhappiness settle on his stomach. He wasn't still in love with her, he told himself, but somehow he didn't want her to get married.

'Is it this murder?' he realized Moira Cartwright was asking him. 'You look quite gloomy.'

'Yes, it is,' lied Hamish. 'I'm hoping one of the locals didn't lose their rag and hit him too hard.'

'Tell me about it.'

So Hamish did and found, as the meal progressed, that he was beginning to relax. She was that rare thing, an excellent listener.

'What puzzles me,' ended Hamish, 'is why no one saw him.'

'I know this seems a bit way out, but if this Fergus got a phone call and went off without telling his wife who he was meeting . . .'

'That wouldn't be unusual. The only communication Martha Macleod had with her husband was the occasional fist in her face.'

'I was going to say he might have been in disguise. But now you've told me about the wife, surely the answer's obvious. She did it. Or someone close to her. You know, murder, like charity, usually begins at home.'

Hamish was about to say stoutly that when Martha hadn't been with him she'd been with

120

Clarry, but that was what he wanted to think. He had slept heavily that night. Clarry could have nipped out if it transpired that Martha really knew where Fergus had gone.

He had not told Moira about the blackmail. But that was one thing he could not keep to himself for much longer.

'What is it?' she asked.

He shrugged. 'Nothing. I just wish it were all over.'

'Have you considered these Currie sisters as suspects?'

'What! That iss ridiculous. Neither of them would hurt a fly.'

'I find you think you know people just because they're under your feet the whole time, so to speak. But there can be a lot of passions burning below the surface.'

'You speak from experience?'

'I was married once. I reverted to my maiden name after the divorce but I still use the "Mrs". Vanity! I don't want to be thought a spinster.'

'What happened?'

'I had a very strict upbringing and John was a bit wild. That was what attracted me. My parents were against it. He turned out a bad lot. He stole cars. Then it was armed robbery. Finally he killed a night watchman. He's out now. Isn't it incredible that somewhere that murdering rat could be walking the streets?'

'Not the streets of Lochdubh, I hope.'

'He doesn't know where I am. It all happened thirty years ago anyway. So what do you lot do for amusement round here when you're not murdering each other?'

'There's no theatre and no cinema, so the younger ones go down to Inverness or over to Strathbane. There's the occasional dance or ceilidh, you know, where we dance and then everyone does something, sings or recites a poem, that sort of thing. Then there's the television.'

'What did they all do to pass the time in the winter before television?'

'They sat around each other's peat fires and told stories. It's an art that's nearly gone. Not many young people stay in the Highlands. It's a place where incomers choose to retire, but often they don't last long. The dark winters usually get to them.'

'I'm not that much of a stranger to the Highlands. I taught over in Dingwall in Cromarty. Lively town, nice people. But I was much younger then, and I wanted to travel. I learned teaching English as a foreign language and then I taught in Italy for a bit, then Japan and then Thailand.'

'Dingwall?' said Hamish. 'Exactly when would that have been?'

'Fifteen years ago.'

'So you wouldn't have been that young.'

'Do you usually shell out compliments like that?'

'Sorry. Tell me more about Dingwall.'

'You know Dingwall. I can't tell you much more. The police there are very good.'

'Have much to do with them?'

She laughed. 'You're beginning to suspect I have a murky past. No, it was nothing like that. Some nasty person sent me a blackmailing letter.'

Hamish sat up straight. 'What about?'

'I was to leave two hundred pounds in ten-pound notes in a bag on a bench at Dingwall railway station at midnight, or the blackmailer would tell everyone that I had been married to a murderer. So I went straight to the police. They got a bag and stuffed it with paper and told me to leave it on the bench as instructed. They kept watch but no one turned up. I didn't hear any more, but it soured Dingwall for me, so I got the job in Edinburgh.'

'Did you have an accountant in Dingwall?'

'What an odd question! No, I had no need of an accountant. I did my taxes myself. Still do.'

Hamish wanted to tell her that Fergus had worked as an accountant in Dingwall, but she would ask if he had continued as a blackmailer, if Fergus had been the one trying to blackmail her in Dingwall, and Hamish did not want to say anything that might betray anyone in Lochdubh.

But he did not believe in coincidences. Here was a schoolteacher who had once worked in

Dingwall, who had been blackmailed. And she had moved to Lochdubh.

'Why?' he asked abruptly. 'Why Lochdubh?'

'I was working in a large comprehensive in Edinburgh. I could have got a job in a private school with smaller classes, but I was still idealistic, thought I could bring my educational skills to those who were not so fortunate in their upbringing.' She sighed. 'It was a nightmare. The pupils were rowdy and noisy. Big loutish boys and girls who had so many parts of their body pierced, they were like walking pin cushions. I stuck it out for quite a while. I didn't make many friends because most of the teachers moved away quite quickly and found work elsewhere, or, after their brutal experiences, left teaching altogether. I became weary. I wanted a quiet life until my retirement. I saw the job was going here and applied for it and got it.'

Hamish thought hard. He wondered if they had dug into Fergus's past properly. He would suggest to Jimmy that a trip to Dingwall might be a good idea.

'That was a lovely meal,' said Moira. 'Next time it's on me.'

'That would be grand,' said Hamish, calling for the bill. 'Look, you might hear or notice something which might relate to the murder. If you hear anything that might be relevant, please let me know.'

* * *

124

With Jimmy's permission, Hamish drove off the following morning to Dingwall with Lugs beside him. The wind had shifted around to the east and it was a bright, cold day.

Dingwall is blessed with convenient car parks at the back of the main street. Hamish drove into one of them, told Lugs to wait, and climbed down from the Land Rover and walked through one of the narrow lanes which led from the car park to the main street.

It is a busy, Highland town with a good variety of small shops, mostly Victorian, grey granite; prosperous, decent and friendly.

Hamish stopped in the main street and took out a piece of paper on which he had noted the name of the firm for which Fergus had once worked: Leek & Baxter, chartered accountants.

The office proved to be above a bakery. He walked up the shallow stone stairs, redolent with the smell of hot bread and sugary buns, and opened a frosted-glass door on the first landing, which bore the legend LEEK & BAXTER in faded gold letters.

Inside, at a desk, an elderly lady was hammering away at an old Remington typewriter. She looked up as Hamish entered, sighed, and then stood up, saying, 'I suppose you want tea.'

'Actually, I came to see one of the partners.'

'Mr Leek is busy and Mr Baxter is out. Mr Leek will be free in ten minutes so you'd better have tea.'

'Thank you.' Hamish sat down on a leather-covered chair. She walked to a kettle in the corner and plugged it in. He watched, amused, as she carefully prepared tea – tea leaves, not bags – and then arranged a small pot, milk jug, sugar bowl and plate with two Fig Newtons on a tray and carried the lot over to him and placed the tray on a low table in front of him.

'Thank you,' said Hamish again.

Her sad old face looked even sadder as she resumed her seat behind the typewriter. 'I missed out,' she said.

'On what?'

'On women's lib, that's what. You won't get the young things these days to make tea.'

'Then you shouldnae do it if you don't want to,' Hamish pointed out.

'I can't stop. I'm the generation that makes tea for men.' She sighed again. Then she said, 'What brings you?'

'Fergus Macleod. Did you know him?'

'Yes, I was here in his day.'

'And what did you make of him?'

'I shouldn't speak ill of the dead.'

'Try.'

'He was a wee scunner and that's a fact. Always complaining and bullying. I got my own back, though.'

'How?'

'He had terrible hangovers, see, and when he had one, I'd wait till he got level with my desk and drop something noisy and make him jump and clutch his head.'

'Why did he get fired? He did get fired, didn't he?'

'It was the drink. He was getting worse, and some days he wouldn't even turn up.'

'Not fiddling the books, was he?'

Her face took on a closed look. 'I wouldn't be knowing about that,' she said. 'If you don't mind, I'll get back to my typing.'

'Why don't you have a computer?'

'I asked them, but they said no, that if they got me a computer they would need to send me on a course, and they couldn't afford to let me have the time off.'

She started to bang away at the keys again. Hamish drank tea and ate biscuits. The door to an inner office opened, and a man came out. He nodded to the secretary, looked curiously at Hamish, and then made his way out. The secretary rose and went into the inner office and closed the door behind her. Hamish could hear the murmur of voices. Outside, somewhere at the back of the building, children were playing, their voices shrill and excited. The fruit crop was late this year, so the children were being allowed extra holidays to help with the picking.

The secretary emerged. 'You're to go in,' she said.

Mr Leek was as old as his secretary, small and stooped with grey hair and gold-rimmed glasses. 'Sit down,' he said. 'I do not know what more I can tell you than I told that detective from Strathbane.'

'I am just trying to build up a picture of Fergus Macleod,' said Hamish patiently.

'He was good enough when we took him on, or rather, he seemed good enough. Then he began to get a reputation as a drunk and then there were too many absences from work, and we had to let him go.'

'That doesn't give me much of a picture of the man. What, for example, did he say when you told him he was fired?'

'Nothing, at that time. He just went.'

'But later?' prompted Hamish.

'He came back a week later, very drunk, and started cursing and threatening and throwing things about the office. I called the police, and he was taken away. But we did not press charges.'

'Was there anything else?'

'Like what?'

'Like fiddling the books?'

'No, nothing like that.'

'Like blackmail?'

There was a silence. 'It's *mine*, it's *mine*,' screamed a child from below the window.

Then Mr Leek said slowly, 'Who told you that?'

'Chust an educated guess,' said Hamish, beginning to feel a buzz of excitement.

'I wouldn't want the poor woman to be bothered.'

'I'll be discreet. But it is important, and you cannae be withholding information from the police.'

'Very well. Her name is Mrs Annie Robinson. He had been having an affair with her, and she was one of our clients. She ended the affair and thought that was that. But he said if she didn't pay him, he would go to her husband and tell him of the affair. She came straight to us. It was enough. We fired him.'

'Did her husband ever find out? Did Fergus get revenge on her?'

'No, he didn't tell her husband. Her husband was a big powerful man. I told Mrs Robinson that Fergus would not dare tell her husband, but she did not believe me, so she told him herself. He divorced her.'

'And where will I find this Mrs Robinson?'

'I suppose I am obliged to tell you. She lives in Cromarty Road, number ten, Invergordon. It's just near the station. She's going to be so upset.'

'I think for Mrs Robinson's sake,' said Hamish cautiously, 'that we should for the moment keep this blackmail matter between ourselves. I will only tell Strathbane if I think it's relevant.'

The interview was over. Hamish shook hands with Mr Leek and made his way out. The secretary was now dusting bookshelves.

'Have you noticed something else about women of my generation?' she said. 'We've aye got a duster or cloth in our hands. Wipe, wipe, wipe, like a nervous tic.'

'You could always change,' pointed out Hamish.

'What? At my age?'

He left her to her dusting and made his way back to the car park. Lugs eyed him sourly when he climbed in.

'Don't look at me like that,' said Hamish severely. 'You'll get a walk after I've finished wi' my business in Invergordon and not before.'

The Land Rover door had been open as he addressed Lugs. A child was standing outside. She then ran away shouting to her mother, 'Mither, there's a daft polisman talking to his dog.'

Hamish reddened and drove off, past where the child was now clutching her mother's skirts.

He found the address in Invergordon, and once more leaving his sulky dog in the vehicle, he knocked at Annie Robinson's door.

A middle-aged woman with one of those faded, pretty faces and no-colour hair opened the door to him. 'Mrs Robinson?'

'I read about his death in the newspapers,' she said, 'and I was frightened you would come.'

'I don't think it's relevant to the case, Mrs Robinson. I'm just trying to build up a picture of Fergus Macleod.'

'You'd best come in.'

The living room was small and dark and very clean. It had a sparse look about it, as if Mrs Robinson could not afford much in the way of the comforts of life.

Hamish removed his cap and sat down. 'Now, then, Mrs Robinson . . .'

'You can call me Annie, everyone does.'

'Right, Annie it is. I am Sergeant Hamish Macbeth. Tell me about the blackmailing business.'

'I'm not . . . I wasn't . . . the sort of woman to have an affair,' she said. 'It's just I didn't know much about men or marriage. My husband, Nigel, always seemed to be complaining. You know. The washing machine would break down, and he would blame me. Everything was always my fault. I know now that men are like that and that's marriage, but I'd grown up on romances. They still pump romance into girls' heads, you know. Nothing about the realities of life. Nothing about men still being aggressive and bullying and fault-finding. Nothing about little facts like when men get a cold, it's flu, when women get a cold it's nothing but a damn cold and what are you whining about? Nothing about being taken for granted. Nothing about the new age for women meaning you have to work and be a slave at home and a tart in the bedroom. Nothing like that.'

'We're not all like that,' said Hamish defensively.

'Are you married?'

'No.'

'Well, there you are. Anyway, I was made redundant from my job. I worked in a dress shop which closed down. Nigel said until I got another one, I could make myself useful and sort out the accounts and take them to the accountants. I met Fergus. He flattered me and flirted with me. He suggested we meet for lunch to discuss the accounts. He encouraged me to complain about my husband and exclaimed in horror over Nigel's treatment. One thing led to another, and we started to have an affair. But I grew tired of the secrecy and the shame. Also, Fergus had hinted that he would marry me, but after I started sleeping with him, he dropped the hints, and I knew he never would. I told him the affair was over. He said he would tell Nigel unless I paid him. I couldn't believe it. I was frightened to death. I told his bosses. I had a letter he had written to me, a threatening letter demanding money. I showed that to them. They were very kind. They said my husband would never know, but I was sure Fergus would tell him. Mr Leek said Fergus would never dare tell Nigel, but I thought Fergus might write to him. I watched the post every morning, dreading the arrival of that letter. It never came but I couldn't stand the shame, the fright, the waiting, and so I told Nigel.

'He said he had always known I was a slut and started divorce proceedings. It was only after the divorce – I'd agreed not to contest it because he said if I did, he'd tell everyone about the affair, and that meant no settlement, no money. So I was on my own, trying to meet the bills, looking for another job. I should never have broken up my marriage.'

'Why?' asked Hamish. 'It sounds to me like a horrible marriage.'

'Other women put up with it.' Her face was crumpled with self-pity.

Hamish's treacherous Highland curiosity overcame him. Instead of sticking closely to the case, he asked, 'But at the beginning of the marriage, the honeymoon period, why didn't you stop his criticisms then? Why did you just let it go on, and why did you run after him, keeping down a job and doing the housework? Couldn't you have asked him to help?'

'You don't know what you're talking about. You ask men to help in the house, and they'll leave you.'

Hamish was about to point out that she was the one who strayed, but he bit the remark back in time. 'So what did you think when you heard about Fergus's death?'

'I assumed he had been up to his old tricks, making some woman's life a misery, and got what he deserved at last. But a dustman! I couldn't believe he had sunk so low.'

'That's what the drink does.'

'I don't want everyone knowing about me and Fergus.'

'I'll do what I can to keep it quiet. Do you know if he was blackmailing anyone else?'

She shook her head.

'Well, if you think of anything that might help, let me know. I'm at the Lochdubh police station.'

'Won't you stay for some tea?'

'No, I have to be going.'

He had a feeling of escape when he walked outside. She had had a hard time, and yet he had not liked her one bit.

He drove a little way and then stopped beside the Cromarty Firth and took Lugs for a walk. He turned the little he knew about the case over and over in his head. He would need to find out who did it quickly or hand those letters over to Strathbane.

He put Lugs in the Land Rover and drove the long way back to Lochdubh, feeling tired when he arrived and hoping for a quiet evening.

Clarry looked up from the kitchen table when he came in. His face was radiant.

'What's happened to you?' asked Hamish. 'Win the lottery?'

'Martha and I are getting married,' said Clarry happily.

Hamish sat down suddenly. 'I'm happy for you, Clarry, but you're going to need to keep quiet about this.'

'Why? I want to tell the world.'

'You'll be telling no one until this case is closed. Blair gets wind o' this, and you'll be suspect number one again. Get round there and tell Martha and the kids to be quiet about it.' The phone rang in the police office. 'I'll get that,' said Hamish. 'Off you go now!'

Hamish ran into the office and picked up the phone. At first he could not make out anything but a screaming babble coming over from the other end. Then he made out a woman's voice shouting, 'It wass the dog. You brought the evil.'

'Kirsty!' he said with a stab of alarm. 'What's happened?'

'He's dead!' she screamed.

'What happened?'

Her voice sank to a whimper. 'Blood. Blood everywhere.'

'I'll be right there.' Hamish slammed down the phone and fled out to the Land Rover.

His heart was beating hard. If this turned out to be another murder, he would need to hand those letters over. He phoned to Strathbane from the Land Rover and reported a suspected murder, hoping all the time that it would turn out to be an accident.

The Land Rover bumped over the heathery track leading to Angus Ettrik's croft. He parked outside the cottage. The door was open. He went inside. Kirsty Ettrik was sitting on the kitchen floor, cradling her husband's bloody head in her hands and keening.

'Get away from him, Kirsty,' ordered Hamish, 'and let me have a look.'

He knelt down on the floor and felt for Angus's pulse. No life. No life at all.

He pulled out his mobile and called Strathbane again and reported a murder. He called for an ambulance, and then called Dr Brodie and told him to come quickly. Then he took Kirsty by the shoulders and lifted her up on to a chair.

'When did you find him?' he asked.

Between sobs, she choked out that she had gone into the village to do some shopping and had returned and found him lying on the kitchen floor.

Dr Brodie was the first to arrive. He examined Angus and then shook his head. 'A murderous blow,' he said.

'Do something about Kirsty then,' said Hamish. 'She's falling apart with shock.'

While the doctor attended to Kirsty, Hamish had a look around the flagged kitchen. A bottle of whisky was open on the table with two clean glasses standing behind it. Angus had been expecting someone. Highland hospitality decreed that the whisky bottle was always left open when a guest was expected.

Kirsty had just swallowed two pills. Hamish went over and crouched down beside her. He said gently. 'Kirsty. Angus was expecting someone. Who was it?'

'He didn't tell me,' she said in a trembling voice. 'He was excited. He said to take myself off and not hurry back. He said our troubles were over.' And she fell to weeping again.

'Leave her,' said Dr Brodie quietly. 'She's too distressed.'

The ambulance arrived. Hamish went out and told the ambulance men they'd have to wait until the police and forensic team arrived. His heart was heavy, but deep inside he still had this stubborn loyalty to the people the horrible Fergus had been blackmailing.

The wail of sirens sounded in the distance. Hamish hoped that Blair was off work, but as the first car swept up, he saw that familiar heavyset figure in the back seat.

It was a long night. If whoever Angus had been expecting had arrived by car, it was difficult to tell, for the heathery rough track leading to the croft had not retained any tyre marks. Dr Brodie said firmly that Kirsty was too deeply in shock to be interviewed further that night and had her taken off to hospital in Strathbane. Blair, furious, tried to protest, but Dr Brodie's decision was backed by the police pathologist.

137

Jimmy Anderson took Hamish aside. 'I dialled 1-4-7-1 on the phone to see if he had any calls, and he had the one, from a call box, the same call box which was used when Fergus got his call. What's going on? Were they friends?'

'He said he had no quarrel with Fergus,' said Hamish. 'This is bad.'

'Aye, they're out combing the countryside, waking up people and asking if they saw a strange car, or any car, heading in this direction. Where's your sidekick?'

'I left him to man the phone at the police station,' lied Hamish, who realized with horror that he had completely forgotten about Clarry. 'We can't get much further, it seems to me, until the wife recovers enough to speak to us.'

'Did you find anything over at Dingwall?'

Hamish realized in that moment that he would need to let something out. He hoped Annie Robinson would forgive him.

'Blackmail!' exclaimed Jimmy. 'Man, now there's something. Say Fergus was murdered for blackmailing someone, and Angus knew who it was, and took over where Fergus left off, it stands to reason we're looking for the same murderer.'

'Aye, it looks like that.'

'So,' said Jimmy, his foxy face alight, 'he could have maybe – Fergus, I mean – have been blackmailing more than one. And how would he have found out anything, hey? By raking through the rubbish to see if folks had got everything into the right containers. Better tell Blair.'

Hamish waited for the inevitable. He was standing outside the cottage when Blair barrelled truculently up to him. 'What's this about that woman over in Invergordon?' he snarled. 'Where's your report?'

'I had just got back and wass going to type it up,' said Hamish, 'when I got the call from Kirsty.'

'You get back down there and start typing. I want all of it. We'll pull her in for questioning.'

Hamish drove off. His heart was heavy. Just because he had not liked Annie Robinson, just because she did not live in Lochdubh, he had turned her over to the police.

Clarry was just returning to the police station when Hamish drove up. 'Get yourself up to Angus Ettrik's,' said Hamish. 'He's been murdered. See if they need you.'

Clarry hurried to his old car, which he kept parked out on the road. Hamish went into the police office, switched on the computer and began to type while the pale dawn rose outside the window. When he had finished, he sent over his report and decided to get some sleep. He washed and changed into civilian clothes and decided to sleep with them on in case he was roused by Blair. Blair would no doubt howl at him for not being in uniform, but he did not want to sleep in all that scratchy

139

serge. With Lugs curled against his side, he fell into a deep sleep, only struggling awake at ten in the morning as he heard a knock at the kitchen door.

The banker's wife, Mrs McClellan, stood there. 'Come in,' said Hamish. 'I was just about to make some coffee. Like some?'

'No, I won't be long. I remembered one little thing.'

'What's that?' asked Hamish, plugging in the kettle. He felt he needed a cup of strong coffee to help him wake up properly.

'The last time Fergus Macleod called to see me, he was quite genial – I mean, he wasn't his usual sneering self. He was bragging how he would soon be getting out of Lochdubh to start a new life. That's it, I'm afraid.'

'Nothing more?'

'No, but it occurred to me that what he might get out of me was hardly enough to enable him to start a new life somewhere else. And it almost seemed as if he had lost interest in what I could give him. I mean, maybe he'd found someone rich.'

'I'd best ask around again,' said Hamish. 'Have you heard? Angus Ettrik has been murdered.'

'The crofter?'

'Himself.'

'That's terrible. What evil's come to Lochdubh?'

'Whatever it is,' said Hamish grimly, 'Fergus Macleod did something to bring it here.'

He had just changed into his uniform when Clarry arrived, tired and unshaven. 'Phew!' he said, sinking down into a chair in the kitchen. 'That Blair had me going round all the outlying crofts. I'm knackered. I told Blair I'd nothing, and he said you were to get out there and go round everyone again.'

Hamish looked gloomily out of the window. A steady drizzle was falling, what the sturdy locals called 'a nice, soft day'.

He put on his oilskin and said to Clarry, 'Do me a favour and walk Lugs, or let him into the garden. I'll probably be away all day.'

Hamish decided to drive up to Elspeth MacRae's croft. She was a widow and ran her croft single-handed. She had a nose for gossip and her land bordered Angus's.

Elspeth was returning home with her dogs just as he drove up. She was a tall, leathery woman with cropped grey hair. 'Bad business, Hamish,' she said, walking up to meet him as he got down from the Land Rover.

'Yes, that's why I'm here. Did you hear anything, notice anything? Anyone calling on Angus?'

141

She shook her head. 'I didn't have much to do with him. We had that row over the peats.'

Hamish nodded. Angus had been digging into Elspeth's peats, and she had complained about him to the Crofting Commission. 'Mind you, Kirsty and I often had a word if he wasn't around. I had no quarrel with her. That fat policeman of yours, the one that's been chasing after Martha Macleod, was up here during the night asking questions.'

'So there's nothing you can tell me?'

'There's someone might help you. I just remembered after your man had gone.'

'And who's that?'

'Sean Fitz is back. He called here two days ago for a cup of tea. He might have called on Angus.'

Hamish brightened. Sean Fitz was the last of the genuine Highland tramps, roving through the mountains and moors.

'I'd best drive around and look for him,' he said. 'Did he say where he was headed?'

'No, but he usually stays around the same area for a bit.'

Hamish drove slowly around the network of single-track roads joining the outlying crofts, and then out on the main Lochdubh–Strathbane road. The rain had stopped and the clouds had rolled back from the mountains. The blazing heather on either side of the road glittered with raindrops. He rolled down the window and breathed in the scent of wild thyme, heather and pine. The magnificence of the glorious landscape reduced the nasty little doings of men to insignificance.

And then, as he crested a hill, he saw the shambling figure of the tramp on the road ahead of him. He drove up and stopped just in front of Sean and jumped down.

Sean was a bearded old man with young eyes in a wrinkled and tanned face. He was dressed in the layers of clothing he wore winter and summer.

Hamish hailed him. 'I need some information, Sean.'

'It wisnae me what took thon trout out o' the colonel's river,' said Sean, backing away.

'I'm not after poachers,' said Hamish. 'Did you know Angus Ettrik had been murdered?'

'Him, too? My, the Highlands are becoming as violent as the cities. I wass up there the ither day. The wife gave me tea and a bit of money for chopping kindling.'

'Did you see Angus?'

'No, he wass out somewheres.'

'Did Kirsty say anything about them maybe getting some money from somewhere?'

'No, Hamish. Herself said as how the bank might be going to take the croft away. She only gave me a wee bit o' money for the work, but I felt right guilty at taking it.'

'You see things. You hear things. You wander around. Let's take Fergus, for instance. Two days before he was found, he disappeared after getting a phone call. No one saw him. No one saw him meet anyone. You didn't see anything?'

Sean hesitated. 'I am not interested in your poaching,' said Hamish sharply. 'I can see by your face that you saw or heard something.'

'If you get me for this, Hamish Macbeth, I'll neffer trust you again.'

'Go on, Sean. I'm getting desperate.'

'I wass up at the river . . .'

'The Anstey?'

'Aye, I was on the colonel's estate . . . You will not be . . .?'

'No, I will not be. Go on, man.'

'I heard the cracking of twigs a bit downstream, and I thought it might be the water bailiff. I was guddling for the trout.'

Hamish nodded. He knew Sean meant that he hadn't a rod; he had been standing in the shallows of the stream, hoping to hook a trout out of the water with his bare hands.

'I moved out of the river and edged back up the bank. Through the trees I could see the pair of them.'

'Who?'

'It wass the colonel and that dustman. The colonel, he wass red in the face. I couldnae hear what wass being said, chust the angry voices. I wass too far away.'

'So what you saw was Colonel Halburton-Smythe and Fergus Macleod having a row?'

144

'Aye, I thought maybe Fergus had been poaching and the colonel had caught him at it.'

'Thanks, Sean,' said Hamish. He dug out his wallet and took out a ten pound note. 'Keep this to yourself. When was this?'

'I'm bad at dates and time, but I 'member it must have been around the time afore Fergus was found, for I 'member reading it in the papers.'

'Anything else?'

'No. Fergus wisnae popular but you must know that yoursel'.'

'Right, Sean. I'll look into it.'

Hamish climbed into the Land Rover, his mind racing. After Fergus's death, the police had appealed for anyone with any information to come forward. The colonel must have heard it.

He drove to the Tommel Castle Hotel. He glanced in at the windows of the gift shop and saw Priscilla behind the counter. He parked the vehicle and walked into the gift shop.

'On your own?' he asked.

'As you can see,' said Priscilla. She was wearing a loose, scarlet cashmere cardigan over a white silk blouse and tailored tweed skirt. The gold bell of her hair framed her calm features. Hamish had a sudden, irrational desire to shake her.

'Where's your friend?'

'Jerry? He's gone back to London.'

145

Hamish glanced covertly at her hands. Ringless.

'Do you want coffee?' Priscilla indicated the coffee machine in the corner.

'No, I'm here on official business.'

She raised a pair of perfect eyebrows.

'Do you get those shaped?' asked Hamish.

'What?'

Hamish flushed slightly. 'Never mind. Is your father about?'

'He's over at the hotel. Why?'

'He was seen by the tramp, Sean, rowing with Fergus Macleod.'

'But that would be about the hotel rubbish. Remember I told you we had to get a private contractor to pick it up?'

'But that was *after* he had disappeared.'

'Hamish, my father is not a murderer.'

'But he was rowing with Fergus and never said a word about it.'

'You know what he's like. Fergus was probably poaching. You all poach. Even you, Hamish.'

'I'll just be having a word with him.'

'That might be a good idea,' said Priscilla coldly, 'instead of talking to me. Unless you think I'm a suspect.'

'No need to get snappy. I'm off.'

'I'll come with you.'

They walked across to the hotel after Priscilla had locked up the gift shop. 'Things quiet?' asked Hamish.

'I'm afraid so. Twelve people from an engineering company had booked in for the fishing, and they cancelled at the last minute. Didn't give any reason. You won't find Daddy in the best of moods.'

'I thought he'd given up bothering about the hotel. I thought he left it all to Mr Johnston.'

'Oh, he gets periods when he swoops down on everyone. Doesn't last long.'

They walked into the reception. 'Is the colonel about?' Priscilla asked the girl behind the reception desk.

'Colonel Halburton-Smythe's round at the back, talking to the gardener.'

They walked through the hotel lounge and through the open French windows to the garden. It was not a flower lover's garden. A huge lawn dipped down to the river, and under the windows were beds with laurel bushes and forsythia and ornamental heather.

'I don't care how wet it's been,' the colonel was shouting. 'I want that lawn mowed now!'

'Daddy!' called Priscilla. The colonel swung round, his angry face relaxing at the sight of his daughter. Then he saw Hamish Macbeth behind her, and his scowl returned.

He walked up to them. 'What is it?'

'Around the time Fergus Macleod disappeared, you were heard down by the river having a row with him.'

The colonel goggled at Hamish, and then he half turned away and stared down the lawn.

'Oh, that? I caught him poaching and sent him off with a flea in his ear.'

Hamish looked at the set of the colonel's shoulders and noticed the way he would not turn directly round to face them, and was sure the colonel was lying.

'It was on the radio and in the newspapers that we were appealing for anyone who had seen or talked to Fergus around the time he went missing, and yet you did not come forward,' said Hamish.

'I'd dealt with the man. I didn't want to get him into trouble over poaching.'

Hamish reflected that the colonel reported every poacher he could catch to the police. 'But Fergus was dead when we made that appeal.'

'It had nothing to do with me!' shouted the colonel. 'If you go on like this, I will report you for police harassment.'

'And if you go on like this,' said Hamish evenly, 'then Detective Chief Inspector Blair will be along to see you.'

'There's no need to make such a to-do about it,' said the colonel, his manner becoming suddenly conciliatory. 'Priscilla, why don't you take Hamish into the bar and get him a drink?'

'I don't need a drink. I'll check with Mrs Macleod as to whether Fergus was in the habit of poaching, and if he wasn't, I'll be back.'

Hamish walked off followed by Priscilla. She caught up with him and said soothingly, 'Don't worry. Whatever it is, I'll get it out of him.'

'Give me a ring right away. I'm sure it's really nothing, but I wish people wouldn't lie to us. They often do over small matters, and all it does is muddy the waters.'

He drove back to Lochdubh, thinking about Priscilla, wishing she would go away again, back to London, and stop this haunting little feeling of something valuable lost.

When Hamish drove up to Martha's cottage, he was glad to see the children playing in the garden. Children were so resilient. If only this murder could be solved and the shadow lifted from Lochdubh. Johnny volunteered the information that his mother was in the kitchen. The door was open, so Hamish walked in. The place looked brighter and lighter already, he thought, and there was a vase of wildflowers on the kitchen table.

'What is it?' asked Martha anxiously when she saw him.

'It is just a little thing, Martha. Was Fergus a poacher?'

'No. I mean he couldn't have been. He never cooked anything for himself, and if he'd caught a fish, he would have had me cook it.

And he didn't like fish at all. He was a meat and potatoes man. What's this about?'

'Fergus was seen up at the Anstey on the colonel's estate. I wondered what he would be doing up there.'

'He often took his bottle off somewhere quiet when he planned to get drunk.'

'Aye, that could be it. How are you getting on?'

'We're doing fine.' She turned a rosy colour. 'Did Clarry tell you . . .?'

'Yes, but I'd keep it quiet at the moment, Martha. You know what folks are like. They might think it odd you getting engaged so soon after your husband's death.'

'I haven't said a word. And I told the children not to say anything.'

'But you're doing fine?'

'As well as can be expected. Everyone's been awfully kind. Angela gave me a red carpet for the bedroom, but it was so nice, I put it in the living room. Brightens things up no end.'

'Take care of yourselves, then. Fergus didn't have any dealing of any kind with the colonel up at Tommel Castle?'

'No, only that the colonel phoned when Fergus was missing and complained about the rubbish not being picked up.'

Hamish left with a heavy heart. The colonel was involved in some way, but Hamish certainly did not feel he could possibly be guilty of murder. Certainly not of double murder. He must work harder, question and question and question, or he would need to turn those letters over to Strathbane. In all his worry, he forgot about the impending visit on the following Wednesday of Mrs Fleming and her dignitaries.

Chapter Six

Now, thieving Time, take what you must –
Quickness to hear, to move, to see;
When dust is drawing near to dust
Such dimunitions needs must be.
Yet leave, O leave exempt from plunder
My curiosity, my wonder!
                    – Mark Antony DeWolfe Howe

Jimmy Anderson called in to the police station that evening. He was unshaven and looked tired.

'Anything?' asked Hamish.

'Just it's beginning to look as if it was done by someone who knew what they were doing. I mean, it was planned.'

'How do you make that out?'

'Any whisky?'

Hamish went to the cupboard and took down the whisky bottle and set it and a glass in front of the detective.

Jimmy poured a glass and leaned back in his chair. 'All the surfaces in that kitchen and the

153

doorknob had been wiped, and he or they, on the way out, wiped the floor behind them as they went.'

'There's something I'd better tell you,' said Hamish. 'The new schoolteacher. It might be important. I think it's nothing. Her name's Moira Cartwright. She was married to a criminal, but a long time ago. She worked in Dingwall and while in Dingwall, she was blackmailed. The police set up a trap but never got the man.'

'So it could have been Fergus?'

'Could have been. Just before he left Dingwall.'

'So why haven't we seen a report on this?'

'Because I couldn't see a motive.' Because, thought Hamish wearily, I'm still protecting the blackmailed of the village. And I promised myself I would only hold on to that information for one day, and now there's been another murder.

'I can see a motive,' said Jimmy. 'You're slipping. She wants a nice wee job up here and comes up aforehand. Bound to have. Got to see the schoolhouse. See where all her stuff will go. Fergus recognizes her. Says if you don't pay up, I'll tell the village about your evil husband.'

'I thought of all that. If she went to the police in Dingwall, then she would have come straight to me.'

'Still, I'd have a word with her.'

'Why isn't Blair here annoying me?'

'He's got to walk on eggshells. That Annie Robinson stuff. Our man didn't find that. You did. Daviot's singing your praises. You aren't holding anything back?'

Hamish longed to tell him about the letters, but once again he promised himself, just one more day.

He shook his head. 'All I can think of is asking and asking. Often there's something that people have seen or heard that didn't seem important at the time. What about that Greek at the hotel? What do we know of him?'

'I've been to see him. So has Blair. Wealthy man. Owns four hotels in Scotland. Makes them pay all right.'

'Any good? His hotels, I mean. Will the new one be competition for the Tommel Castle Hotel?'

Jimmy gave his foxy grin. 'I know you, Hamish Macbeth, and I know the way that Highland brain of yours is working. You're praying it's some outsider. Nasty foreign hotel owner plans to ruin the Tommel Castle, so Fergus finds out and blackmails owner and owner hires goons to bump him off.'

Hamish gave a reluctant grin. 'Aye, that would suit me just fine. I'm beat. Is there any hope of getting any sleep tonight?'

'If the press leave you alone. But they're mostly badgering headquarters in Strathbane. That Fleming woman got herself on television at last. She turned up at the press briefing and made a speech. Daviot was furious.'

'Wish it would turn out to be her,' said Hamish gloomily.

'Where's your man?'

'Clarry's gone out to interview more people. He's wasted in the police force. He's such a grand cook. He's left my dinner in the oven.'

'What is it?'

'Coq au vin.'

'Enough for two?'

'Knowing Clarry, I should think there's enough for a regiment. Want some?'

'Aye. Got any wine to go with it?'

'No.'

'I'll nip along to Patel's and get us something.'

When Jimmy returned, Hamish gave them each two large helpings from the casserole. 'This is magic,' said Jimmy. 'Is Clarry still courting the widow?'

'Who said anything about that?' demanded Hamish sharply.

'Everyone in the village, that's who.'

'They're just friends.'

'Listen tae me, Hamish Macbeth, you keep going on as if you're a sheriff in a Wild West movie, a one-man law officer. But one day you'll hold back stuff and someone will get hurt.'

Hamish's conscience smote him. Maybe if he had told them about the letters, Angus would be alive. But then, he was sure Angus had been blackmailing someone, someone Fergus had told him about. Then it could be argued that if the blackmailing had been out in the open, then Angus would not have even tried. Suddenly, with a forkful of food halfway to his mouth, he remembered that tiny thread of pink he had found in the Curries' fence. Damn, he would ask them about it first and then send it to Strathbane.

After Jimmy had left, Hamish ignored Lugs's pleading. 'No coq au vin for you,' he said severely. 'The bones are too soft for ye and the food's too rich, and you've had your dinner. Bed for us.'

He left a note on the table thanking Clarry for the dinner, washed, undressed and got into bed. Lugs leapt up beside him. Hamish stroked the dog's rough fur. He would need to see the Curries in the morning and then the colonel again. He fell straight down into a nightmare that he was in Chief Superintendent Daviot's office being asked why it was that he had held back vital information from the police. 'If it had not been for this,' said Daviot, 'then that crofter might still have been alive.'

Hamish awoke, feeling as if he had not slept at all. He wearily washed and dressed and then selected a new toothbrush from the whole packet of them that he had bought, and scrubbed his teeth. This definitely was the very last day, he told himself. Just one more day and then those letters would go to Strathbane.

He and Clarry had a silent breakfast. Hamish was worried about the case and Clarry was worrying that the murder would never be solved, and if it were not, he feared that Martha would not marry him. 'I don't like this shadow hanging over us,' she had told him. 'I feel I can't even be seen with you until the murderer is found.'

Hamish took Lugs for a walk along the waterfront. It was still August, but there was already a chill in the air, a harbinger of the long dark northern winter to come.

He took Lugs back to the police station, collected the envelope with the little bit of pink thread in it and then approached the Curries' cottage. He saw the curtains twitching as he walked up the garden path, and Nessie opened the door to him before he could ring the bell.

'What is it now?' she asked.

Hamish took out the envelope and showed her the little scrap of thread. 'I found this caught in that fence of yours at the side. Could it have come from any of your clothes?'

'No, we have nothing pink. Wouldn't be seen dead wearing pink at our age.'

'What about blankets or sheets or towels?'

She shook her head. 'Nothing pink at all.'

'And you haven't remembered anything that might be of help?'

'Not a thing. All the gossip's about Josie cancelling the wedding. Jilted that fiancé of hers at the last minute! I don't know what girls these days can be thinking about.'

'She jilted him?'

'That's what she's saying. Her mother came round to return our present. I said to Jessie, I said, we'll just put it away safe and keep it for the next wedding, but I don't know when that'll be. Nobody gets married these days, not even you, Hamish Macbeth.'

Hamish made his escape. He collected the Land Rover and drove up to the Tommel Castle Hotel. Every time he arrived at the hotel, he could not help remembering the days when it had been a private house, the days before the colonel had invested wildly and badly and lost everything. Although he had suggested to the colonel that he might consider the idea of turning his home into a hotel, the colonel had never given him any credit for the suggestion.

Priscilla was crossing the entrance hall with a sheaf of papers in her hands when he walked in. 'Your father around?' asked Hamish.

'Oh, Hamish, he's gone off to stay with friends. He didn't say where he was going.'

'What about your mother?'

'She's gone with him.'

159

Hamish clucked his tongue in annoyance. 'I've got to find him. Did you get anything out of him?'

'No, he says Fergus was poaching.'

'Fergus didn't even like fish, Priscilla. Your father's lying.'

'So you say.'

'Oh, Priscilla, this is important. If he phones, find out where he is. I've got to talk to him.'

'I can't think he would have anything to do with this. Have you considered that Fergus might have been at the river to find a quiet place to get drunk? And that Daddy might just have assumed he was poaching? He thinks that everyone near that river is poaching. He once bawled out an innocent family of picnickers.'

'Could be. But I'd still like to speak to him.'

Priscilla's face took on a closed look. Hamish surveyed her for a moment and then said gently, 'You know something's wrong, Priscilla. Please try to help me on this one. Two men are dead.'

'I'll do my best,' she said stiffly. 'Now, if you'll excuse me, Hamish, we've just had new bookings to replace the ones we lost, so I've got to get on.'

Hamish left and then wondered what to do next. He rang Jimmy Anderson's mobile. 'Is Kirsty Ettrik ready to see anyone yet?'

'No, she's still heavily sedated, and the doctors won't let anyone near her. I'm up at

Angus's croft. We're still looking for clues. I think you should still keep going round the village from door to door, Hamish. Someone must have seen or heard something.'

Hamish rang off. He decided to call on Josie Darling again.

Josie answered the door to him. Her face was blotchy with tears. 'It's you,' she said in a bleak voice. 'I heard about Angus.'

He followed her in. 'I gather you've been telling everyone that you jilted Murdo.'

'I wasn't going to let everyone know the rat had jilted me,' she said. 'It was going to be such a beautiful wedding.'

'Josie, I want you to think about Fergus's visits to you. Didn't you threaten to go to the police?'

'I didn't. I was too ashamed. It's all Darleen McPhee's fault.'

'Who's Darleen McPhee?'

'She's a girl I work with in the bank.'

'So what's she got to do with it?'

'She was always bragging about her boy-friends and hinting that I'd never get a man. The day I walked in with my engagement ring and flashed it in front o' her stupid face was the best day o' my life. I couldn't let her know I'd been jilted. Now I've got to go back to work and tell her the wedding's off.'

Fergus must have been acute enough to guess at such desperate vanity, thought Hamish.

'Tell me about Fergus,' he said. 'What was his manner when you last saw him?'

She sank down in a chair and scrubbed at her eyes with a grimy handkerchief. 'He was different,' she said at last.

'What d'ye mean, "different"?'

'Well, joking, excited. Funny, that was the only time he didn't ask for the money.'

Hamish's hazel eyes sharpened. That could only mean one thing. Fergus was blackmailing someone with real money. His heart sank as he thought of the colonel. But then he reflected that there was no way the colonel would kill anyone. Somehow he believed that the murders had been planned. Dumping Fergus's body in the bin, he was sure, smacked more of revenge than any effort at concealment. Whoever put the body there could not know that the Currie sisters rarely put rubbish in the bin, that they recycled what they could.

He thanked Josie and left and drove to Callum McSween's croft. Callum was out in the fields with his sheep. Hamish waved to him, vaulted a fence and walked across the springy turf to join him. There is very little arable farming in Sutherland. The land is mostly used for sheep rearing because the hard old rock which makes up most of Sutherland is only covered with a thin layer of soil.

'I'm getting ready for the sales in Lairg,' said Callum. 'Thank God I've got the rubbish job because sheep prices have been dropping like a stone.'

'You go around the crofts and houses. What's the gossip about Angus's murder?'

'They're all shocked. We all thought we knew Angus, but no one really knew him that well. He must have said something to Kirsty.'

'We'll need to wait until she recovers a bit,' said Hamish. 'Keep listening, Callum, and let me know if you hear anything.'

As he made his way back to the police station, he reflected on the oddity of the case. How could a man walk out to meet someone in the Highlands and not be noticed? Fergus must have been seen in Lochdubh. Unless, of course, he had walked straight up through the grazing land at the back of where his cottage lay and met someone up on the hill.

When he got back to the police station, Clarry called from the police office: 'Is that you, sir? Anderson's on the phone.' Hamish went through and took the receiver from Clarry.

'I'm down in Strathbane,' said Jimmy, 'and I'm a bit tied up. I want you to go and talk to that schoolteacher. Find out if Cartwright is her married name and what her husband's name was. It's all a bit odd. You see, I checked with the police in Dingwall, and they have no record at all of any trap to catch a blackmailer. I checked the schools in Dingwall as well, and there's no record there of a Mrs Cartwright ever having been employed as a teacher.'

'Why would she lie?'

'That's something you'd better find out, and quick, too.'

'Why's Blair leaving me in peace? It hasn't ever mattered before what Daviot said. He likes to rile me.'

'He's in hospital.'

'Nothing trivial, I hope?'

'Something up with his kidneys.'

'The whisky is what's up with his kidneys. I'll get on to the schoolteacher right away.'

'I'm going out again,' Hamish called to Clarry. 'Could you take Lugs for a walk?'

'I've got to get some shopping. I'll take him with me.'

Hamish walked along to the cottage next to the school and rapped on the door. Moira Cartwright answered it. 'Come in,' she said. 'How are you getting on with the case?'

He followed her into the living room of the cottage, removed his peaked cap and sat down.

'I'm here to find out why you told me that story about the blackmail attempt in Dingwall,' he began.

'Would you like some tea?'

'No, just answer the question. The police in Dingwall have no record of any trap set up for a blackmailer fifteen years ago, nor is there any record of you having ever taught in Dingwall. So were you lying?'

There was a long silence. The wind had started to rise outside, the vicious wind of Sutherland that whipped across the county with ferocious force.

Then she said, 'Yes.'

'Why on earth?'

'Do I have to tell you?'

'Of course you have to tell me. Headquarters have been checking up, and they want an answer.'

'I'm a fantasist. Anyway, when I saw the look on your face when you walked into that restaurant, I guessed you had made a mistake, that you had seen my niece and thought she was the schoolteacher.'

'So you decided to waste police time and present me with a red herring?'

'Yes.'

Hamish studied her face and then said slowly, 'You're still lying. And I am going to stay here until you tell me the truth.'

She looked at him helplessly and then said, 'If I tell you, she'll never forgive me.'

'Who?'

She gave a helpless shrug. 'Fiona McClennan.'

'The banker's wife?'

She nodded.

Hamish took out his notebook. 'Begin at the beginning and go on to the end.'

'We're old school friends. We both went to school in Edinburgh. We wrote to each other from time to time. I finally wrote and said I was taking the job in Lochdubh. She phoned me up. She said I wasn't to tell a soul but she was being blackmailed and told me about it. I told her to go to the police, but she said her husband couldn't bear another scandal. I called on her just after I arrived. She said she had told you and that you were trying to keep it quiet for a bit. But I thought, she'll never be happy until the murderer is caught and how can you go about finding the murderer if you didn't know Fergus was a blackmailer, so I decided to tell you I had been blackmailed.'

'But you must have known we would check!'

'I didn't think the police records at a wee place like Dingwall would go back that far.'

'The police in Dingwall cover quite a large area. They're sharp and efficient and, yes, they keep files. How could you have been so stupid? All you've done is force me to tell the police about Mrs McClellan. And how am I going to get you out of being charged with wasting police time?'

Tears welled up in Moira's eyes. 'I was only trying to help.'

'I can tell you this, if I don't get a break today, tomorrow is the longest I can hold this report. Now, that criminal husband of yours. Was that a lie as well?'

'No, I use my maiden name. His name was John Sampson.'

'I'll forget about him for the moment and see what I can do during the rest of the day. You'll just need to hope I find someone.'

'Maybe I can help.'

'No,' said Hamish sharply. 'You've done enough damage.'

'What'll I tell Fiona?'

'Nothing at the moment. Pray.'

Hamish went back to the police station, went through to the office, sat down at his desk and buried his head in his hands. He needed to think things through. Angus was dead. Had Fergus confided in Angus? Had Angus, desperate to keep the croft, decided to go on where Fergus had left off? By tomorrow, he would really need to put in a full report to Strathbane, turn over the letters and put in a report about the colonel as well. They would want to see Sean, to interrogate him as well, and would wonder why Hamish had just let him go on his way. He stood up. He would need to find Sean and tell him to report to the police station in the morning. He could only hope the tramp had decided not to leave the area.

He went out and got in the police Land Rover and drove off. He went back to the place where he had found Sean the day before and then started to slowly cruise along, looking to right and left. Then he remembered that the village of Drim was one of Sean's favourite places, and he turned the vehicle and headed towards the Drim road.

Once in Drim, he parked outside the general store. Ailsa Kennedy was behind the counter. Hamish waited until she had served a customer and then asked, 'Have you seen the tramp, Sean Fitz?'

'What's he done?' asked Ailsa.

'Nothing. I just want a wee word with him.'

'I saw him a while ago. He's probably at one of the houses.'

Hamish patiently set off, calling at cottage after cottage, until he found the tramp sitting outside a house, a mug of tea in one hand and a large sandwich in the other. 'Oh, it's yourself, Hamish,' he said.

'Look, Sean, you'll need to promise me you'll come to the police station tomorrow morning. I'm going to have to put in a report about the colonel, whether he likes it or not.'

'Och, Hamish, that bugger Blair'll have me locked up in Strathbane for questioning. He'll hae me for being on the colonel's river.'

'He can't. Just say you were wandering around. I need you, Sean.'

'I tell you something, I'd like a soft bed for the night.'

'All right. You know where the cell is. Come and stay the night, and we'll deal with it in the morning.' Hamish sat down beside Sean and heaved a sigh. 'I tell you, Sean, it's not just the colonel I've been covering up for, it's other people as well, and now I feel bad about it.'

Sean drank his tea and munched his sandwich. Then he said, 'Has it no' dawned on you, Hamish, that you won't maybe be the only one keeping quiet to protect people? Say someone in Lochdubh actually saw Fergus talking to someone, a friend of theirs. They wouldnae be giving you the name.'

Hamish thought about that. The villagers would certainly close ranks to protect someone they knew and liked. But he had questioned and questioned.

'I've asked and asked, Sean. Why should anyone tell me now?'

'You could trick them. Let them think you know.'

'But who?'

'Well, laddie, if anyone in Lochdubh's going to notice, it's them Currie sisters.'

'Come on, Sean. They report everything.'

'Maybe not.'

Hamish looked at him sharply. 'If you know something, Sean, you'd better tell me. I'm getting desperate.'

'Chust an educated guess.'

Hamish rose to his feet. 'I'll see you this evening, Sean.'

'Aye, grand.'

As Hamish walked down to the waterfront and got in the Land Rover, he turned what Sean had said over in his mind. Then he phoned the station to see if there had been any messages. Clarry answered the phone. He sounded excited. 'That friend o' yours, Priscilla, was here. Her chef has just walked out, and she asked me if I could help out at the hotel with the dinners.'

'Clarry, we're in the middle of two murder investigations.'

'I could do it. I know I could.'

'I'll call at the castle and then I'll let you know.'

Hamish set off and drove to the Tommel Castle Hotel. As he parked, he could see Priscilla's blonde head in the gift shop. The car park was full of cars. Business must have picked up.

'Did Clarry tell you . . .?' began Priscilla when Hamish walked in.

'Aye. I'll do a deal with you, Priscilla. You find that father of yours and get him to tell me the truth about why he was rowing with Fergus, and I'll send Clarry up.' He carefully studied her blank face and exclaimed, 'You know where he is!'

Priscilla looked down and fiddled with some Scottish silver jewellery she had been unpacking.

He eyed her for a moment. 'I want you to get your father for me, Priscilla. I'll have to put in a report about him, so either he deals with me or he deals with Blair.'

He left the shop and crossed the car park, went into the hotel and walked into the office. 'What brings you?' asked Mr Johnston.

'Do you know where the colonel is?'

He shook his head. 'We're in too much of a mess at the moment. We need a chef for this evening. Did Priscilla tell you to ask that man of yours?'

'Yes, and I told her, no colonel, no Clarry.'

'What's he done?'

'Probably nothing. But he was seen having a row with Fergus, down by the river. Any idea what it would be about?'

'No. I'm too worried about the chef to think about anything else.'

'I might have another word with Heather Darling. Is she on duty?'

'She's left.'

'Why?'

'Didn't say.'

'I'd better go and see her.'

When Hamish drove off, he could see Priscilla working in the shop. What had happened to the days when they used to discuss his cases? Somewhere inside her, she had retreated even further from him.

He was driving slowly along the waterfront when he saw Nessie Currie working in her garden. He stopped and climbed down.

'Lazing about as usual?' asked Nessie, stooping to pull out a weed.

That remark irritated Hamish enough for him to say angrily, 'I believe you're hiding something from me.'

'And what makes you think that?' she demanded tartly.

But there was a certain shiftiness about her that made Hamish decide to use Blair's tactics. 'If you'll chust step along to the station with me,' he said.

'Why? Why should I?'

'I want to take down a statement from you that you never saw Fergus Macleod on the night he was killed, and I want you to swear on the Bible that you are telling the truth!'

She stared up at him, her eyes magnified by her thick glasses. Hamish stared back, his normally genial face hard and set.

'You'd best come in the house.'

Hamish followed her in. 'Where's your sister?'

'Along at Patel's.'

Hamish removed his cap, sat down and took out his notebook. 'Right, Nessie, let's have it.'

'I didn't want to get him into trouble, such a decent wee man.'

'Who?' demanded Hamish.

'Archie Maclean.'

'And when and where was this?'

'It must've been the night Fergus was killed. I went up the back for a bit o' fresh air. I saw them up on the grazing.'

'Were they arguing? Fighting?'

'No.'

'And then what?'

'Fergus went away over the back, and Archie walked down past the house here.'

'Why the hell didn't you tell me this afore?'

'It wasn't important.'

'A man's murdered and you're the only witness for that evening, and you thought it wasn't important?'

'There's no need to shout at me like that, Hamish Macbeth. I used my intelligence, which is something you should try. Archie Maclean. As decent a body that ever lived in Lochdubh.'

'I want you to come to the police station tomorrow and make a statement.'

'Why tomorrow?'

Because tomorrow, thought Hamish, I bring the whole house of cards, of subterfuge and cover up, down around the ears of everyone.

'Because I'm busy today,' he said stiffly.

He drove to the police station and left the Land Rover and then went in search of Archie. Archie Maclean, he thought bleakly. Archie with his tight suit and bullying wife was part of the scenery of Lochdubh. He was a kind and gentle man. But just what if Fergus had found something out about him and threatened to tell Mrs Maclean? The only thing in the whole wide world that frightened Archie was his wife.

When he saw Archie sitting on the harbour wall, he wondered for the first time when Archie slept. He went out fishing at night but was often to be seen wide awake around the village during the day.

'Archie!' Hamish hailed him. 'A word with you.'

'What about?' asked Archie amiably. He rolled a cigarette, popped it in his mouth, lit it and inhaled smoke. Hamish had a sudden sharp longing for a cigarette.

'I have a witness, Archie, that saw you up on the grazing land on the night Fergus was murdered, and you were seen talking to him.'

'Oh, aye? And chust who saw me?'

'Never mind. Chust answer my question. Did you speak to Fergus?'

'Aye.'

'You'd better tell me about it, Archie. This is bad.'

'I wasnae going to be dragged down tae Strathbane and grilled over that dustman. I had nothing to do with his death.'

'Tell me what happened.'

'The wife's been after me for drinking. I chust wanted a wee dram in peace and quiet afore I went out with the boat. I thought I'd get a half bottle from Patel's and go up to the grazings. Nice and quiet up there. I was sitting in the heather when I saw Fergus, all dressed up, coming towards me.

'"Sneaking a dram,"' he jeered. '"Bet your missus would like to know about it."'

'So I stood up, and I told him what I thought of him. I called him a nasty bugger. I said the whole village hated him. He chust laughed in that sneering way o' his and said, "Cheer up. I'll soon be leaving the lot of you." Then he headed up through the grazing.'

'Any idea where he was going?'

'No.'

'Was he sober?'

'Stone cold and nasty with it.'

'I'll need to get back to you, Archie. You should have told me this.'

Hamish went back to the police station. 'Priscilla phoned,' said Clarry. 'She says her father will see you at seven o' clock this evening.'

'Good.'

'So I can go?'

'What?'

'The cooking?'

'Oh, sure. But I want you to go first up to the grazings.' Hamish told him about Archie Maclean. 'Start searching. See if there's any sign of blood. Except we're too late. The rain'll have washed anything away. But try to find something that might point to where he was heading. I'll join you shortly. First, I want a word with someone.'

As he walked up to the Darlings' cottage, Hamish heard his stomach rumbling. He was hungry, but this little break had excited him. Food could wait.

There was no answer at the cottage. He stood still for a moment. He felt sure there was someone inside. He turned and walked away out through the garden gate and down the brae. He went a few yards and then whipped round and stared up at the cottage. A curtain twitched.

He marched back up to the cottage door and called through the letter box: 'Police! I know you're in there. Open up.' Then he waited.

After a few moments, the door opened and Heather Darling peered nervously up at him.

'Why didn't you answer the first time I knocked?' asked Hamish.

'The washing machine was working in the kitchen,' said Heather. 'I thought I heard something, but I wasn't sure.'

'Can I come in?'

She stood back reluctantly and then turned around and led the way into the living room.

'What's this about you leaving the Tommel Castle Hotel?'

'I don't see what that's got to do with the police,' said Heather defiantly. 'But the fact is

I need a rest. Josie's gone back to the bank, and she's got a bittie o' a rise, so she asks me to turn in my job.'

Hamish studied her face and then said simply, 'You're lying. Somehow I feel that everyone has been lying to me about this and that. Come on, Heather, what happened? Did you have a row with the colonel?'

'I'm telling you, I just needed a rest.'

'And I'm telling you,' roared Hamish suddenly, 'that you are lying and God help me when I find out why.'

And that, he thought privately, was a performance worthy of Blair.

She gave a little shrug and sat down. 'I don't like to seem disloyal,' she said. 'Them up at the castle have been good to me.'

'And what does that all mean?'

'I'm starting work at the new hotel in two weeks' time.'

'Why?'

'It's all modern and posh.'

Hamish sat down and eyed her shrewdly. 'More money?'

'Aye, a fair bit more. Anyway, what's it to do with you where I work?'

'Nothing. But when you don't answer the door at first and then you lie to me, I begin to wonder what's behind it. Look here, Heather, I have to keep asking questions and following up everything because time is passing fast and if I don't get something today, that letter to

Josie from Murdo that was found at Fergus's cottage will have to go to the police.'

'Now that everyone knows the wedding's off,' said Heather, 'Josie won't mind so much.'

'Are you sure you're making a good move?' asked Hamish. 'I mean, the Halburton-Smythes are good employers. You don't know about this new lot.'

'I've got to take a chance.'

'But if other staff start to leave, the Halburton-Smythes may be ruined.'

'Maybe if they put up the wages, I'll go back.'

'Have you looked into this thoroughly? I mean, what are the working terms? Have you any sort of contract? What happens if they suddenly decide to sack you?'

'I'm a good worker.'

'So there's good pay and good benefits. How long do they give you for holidays?'

'They said they would discuss all that sort of thing after I had started. You've got to see it from their point of view. They say all new staff will be on a month's trial.'

'Surely it's not usual to put a hotel maid on a month's trial?'

'This is big business, you see,' said Heather naively. 'Mr Ionides has hotels all over the place. He says if we're good workers, he'll even give us a chance of working in one of his foreign hotels.'

'I would be careful if I were you,' said Hamish, 'and try to get some sort of written agreement. Tommel Castle won't be anxious to have you back after they've gone to all the trouble to replace you.'

'It'll be fine. You should see the bedrooms. Gold taps on the bath, pink sheets on the bed. Grand, it is.'

'And how did they approach you?'

'I got a letter asking me to come for an interview.'

'How did they know where you live?'

She looked puzzled and then she said, 'Oh, you know what this village is like. Everyone knows where everyone else lives.'

'Promise me you'll see them again and ask them for some proper arrangement.'

A flash of Highland malice gleamed in Heather's eyes. 'We all know you have a special interest in the Halburton-Smythes.'

'That's enough of that,' said Hamish stiffly. 'Chust take my advice.'

He left Heather's cottage and then stood outside the garden gate, looking down at the new hotel by the harbour.

He had dismissed the proprietor of the hotel from his mind because he knew Ionides had been thoroughly interviewed by detectives. Now he was suddenly anxious to see the man for himself.

He marched down to the hotel and into the new hotel reception area. He headed for the door marked OFFICE, knocked and went in. An attractive woman was working at a computer. 'Is it possible to see Mr Ionides?' asked Hamish.

She stopped typing. 'What about?'

'The murders, of course.'

'Mr Ionides is tired of his valuable time being taken up, being interviewed over two murders in this village.'

'Nonetheless, I wish to see him.'

She carefully saved what she had been typing on the computer and went into the inner office.

Hamish looked around at the well-equipped secretary's room. There were filing cabinets, fax machine, laser copy machine and three phones on the desk. The door opened and the secretary said, 'He can spare you a few moments.'

Hamish went into the inner office. Mr Ionides rose from behind a Georgian rosewood desk. 'You are . . .?'

'Sergeant Hamish Macbeth of Lochdubh.'

'Ah, yes, please sit down.'

Hamish sank his long form down into a low chair in front of the desk. He wondered if the chair was deliberately low so that anyone facing the Greek owner would be at a psychological disadvantage.

He studied the owner. He saw a small dapper man with smooth hair and liquid brown eyes. His chalk-striped suit was double-breasted, and he wore a red silk tie with a red silk handkerchief in his jacket pocket.

'I am investigating the murders in Lochdubh,' began Hamish. 'Have you or your staff seen any strangers in the area?'

'I have been asked this question before,' said Mr Ionides. 'Apart from myself and Miss Stathos, no.'

'And you plan to use local staff?'

'That is the idea. I always use local staff.'

'I gather you plan to take staff from the existing hotel.'

Mr Ionides shrugged. 'Why not? I need the help and all's fair in love and the hotel business. There's not that many jobs going up here in the Highlands. The Tommel Castle will soon find replacements, should they need them.'

'Why here?' asked Hamish abruptly. 'Why Lochdubh?'

'Fishing,' said Mr Ionides simply. 'I am a passionate fisherman – deep sea fishing, freshwater fishing, the lot.'

'But the best fishing is on the River Anstey, and the colonel has the fishing rights.'

'I can buy a permit. Now, is there anything else?'

'I would appreciate your help. If you can think of anything or hear anything which might relate to the murders, I would be grateful.'

'I will tell Miss Stathos to let you know. Now if you don't mind, I have a busy schedule.'

Hamish stared at him, his face quite vacant as he tried to think of something else. Ionides regarded him with amusement.

Hamish then struggled out of the depths of his chair and stood up. 'Thank you for your time,' he said.

He made his way out. Once outside and back in the hotel foyer, he suddenly stood still and listened. He heard Ionides's voice: 'Anna, I think there must be inbreeding in this part of the world. That policeman looked half-witted.'

Hamish strode out of the hotel and went straight to the station and into the office. He decided to try to find out more about Ionides. Then he remembered Chief Inspector Olivia Chater in Glasgow. He reached for the phone and then hesitated. They had worked on a case together, had an affair, but she had left him to go back to Glasgow. Still, business was business and Olivia was one of the best detectives he knew. He phoned Glasgow and asked to be put through to her. After a few moments, a man came on the line and said, 'This is Detective Constable George McQueen. I gather you're asking for Chief Inspector Chater.'

'Yes.'

'Who are you?'

'Sorry. I'm Sergeant Hamish Macbeth of Lochdubh in Sutherland. We worked on a case together.'

'I'm afraid Olivia's dead.'

Hamish clutched the phone. 'Dead?' he echoed. 'What happened?'

'Cancer.'

'Cancer?' Hamish felt engulfed by a sad bleakness. If only she had phoned, he could have been there for her.

'When did she die?' he asked.

'Must have been about three months ago. I'm sorry to have to give you such bad news.'

With a great effort, Hamish rallied. 'We have two murders up here.'

'Aye, so I heard.'

'Now there's a hotel owner here, Ionides. Would you have anything on him?'

'Hang on, I'll check the computer.'

Hamish waited and thought miserably of Olivia. He had wanted to marry her, and yet he had forgotten her so easily.

At last the detective came back on the line. 'There's a smell about the man, but he's never been charged with anything.'

'What do you mean, "a smell"?'

'Well, he wanted to buy a hotel out Aberfoyle way, but the owner didn't want to sell. Then things started happening.'

'Like what?'

'The hotel had a good chef. He left and sub-sequently reappeared working at one of

Ionides's hotels, the one in Glasgow. Then the other staff started to disappear. Then the hotel was closed down after a health scare. Cockroaches found in the kitchen. The owner lost so much business he was forced to sell out to Ionides and at a cheap price, but we couldn't prove anything. Then in Stirling, there was the business of the illegal immigrants. When he started up there, it was all local staff and soon after they started work, they were replaced by foreigners – Filipinos, I think they were. Got a buzz they hadn't work permits and raided the place. Turned out to be the case. Somehow Ionides got off with it. Claimed he hadn't known, that they had said they would supply the documents, and since they had all been recently hired, the sheriff let him off. That's all I've got.'

Hamish thanked him and rang off. If, he thought, his mind racing, Ionides had been into dirty tricks before and planned some more in Lochdubh and Fergus had found out, what a ripe source of blackmail. What had he found? A letter? Perhaps a fax. Ionides wouldn't e-mail any planned campaign against the Tommel Castle Hotel in case his e-mail got hacked into.

Clarry appeared and said nervously, 'I'm off to do my cooking at the hotel.'

'All right,' said Hamish absently.

'Do you think I can do it? I've never cooked on a large scale before.'

'You'll be fine. I'll see you later, maybe. I've got to talk to the colonel. Has Lugs been fed?'

'Yes, and walked. He's sleeping in his basket.'

Clarry left. Hamish phoned Mr Johnston, the manager of the Tommel Castle Hotel. 'Can you give me the address of that chef who walked out on you?'

'Wait a minute, Hamish, and I'll look for you.'

Hamish waited patiently. Then Mr Johnston came back on the phone. 'He's living in that bed and breakfast, Mrs Ryan's, down by the bridge.'

'Right. What's his name?'

'Jeff Warner.'

Hamish thanked him and rang off.

He got in the Land Rover and drove to Mrs Ryan's boarding house. Mrs Ryan answered the door to him and said that Jeff was in his room. 'Just show me which one,' said Hamish. She led the way up the narrow wooden staircase, her carpet slippers, worn down at the back, flip-flopping on the treads. 'Is he in trouble?' she asked. 'I keep a decent house.'

'No, no trouble at all,' said Hamish.

'That's his room.'

'Right.' Hamish knocked at the door and called. 'Police.'

A squat, burly man answered the door. He reeked of whisky. 'What's up?' he asked.

'I chust want a word with you,' said Hamish, aware that the landlady was listening avidly.

'Come in.'

The room was small and sparsely furnished. There was a narrow bed in one corner covered in a pink candlewick bedspread, one easy chair, a small television set, a wardrobe and a washstand basin.

'What d'ye want?' asked Jeff.

'You left the Tommel Castle Hotel?'

'So what? That a crime?'

'I want you to tell me if you have been offered a job at the new hotel.'

'Why?'

Hamish was tired and Hamish was hungry. 'Chust tell me!' he shouted.

'Och, well, what's the harm in it? I'm a good chef and the new lot offered me more money.'

'But the new hotel isn't open yet.'

'Aye, but they're paying me until I start, and it's a damn sight more than that tight-arsed colonel was giving me.'

'I want you to come down to the station tomorrow morning to make a statement to that effect.'

'Whit is this, man? I mean, whit's wrong wi' me wanting a better job?'

'Chust do as you are told.'

'Oh, all right. But it seems daft to me.'

Hamish left him and went out to the Land Rover. He was about to climb in when he suddenly froze. Pink. The thread he had taken from the fence at the Curries' had been pink. Heather had said there were pink sheets in the new hotel rooms. Jeff's bedspread had been pink. Then he climbed in. Colonel Halburton-Smythe was going to have to talk.

Chapter Seven

To-morrow, and to-morrow, and to-morrow,
Creeps in this petty pace from day to day,
To the last syllable of recorded time;
And all our yesterdays have lighted fools
The way to dusty death.
                    – William Shakespeare

As Hamish returned to the police station, he could hear a whirring sound coming closer. He shielded his eyes and looked up at the sky. A helicopter was coming in to land behind the hotel. There was only the pilot in it.

He phoned Jimmy Anderson. 'Look, there's been a bit of a new development. Is there any chance of getting a search warrant for the new hotel?'

'You'd need a rock solid reason. What is it?'

'It's just that I've been given the impression that Fergus thought he was on to big money, and the only big money around is Ionides, the new owner.'

'And that's all you've got?'

'Well, not only that, but he's got a shady record.'

'But nothing criminal. We went into all that. I told you, Hamish, you're that desperate it should turn out to be an outsider that you're clutching at straws. The answer is no, sonny, and there's something else you should be thinking of.'

'What's that?'

'If he thought he had a big cheese to blackmail, why aren't you thinking of Colonel Halburton-Smythe?'

Hamish fell silent.

'Well?' demanded Jimmy. 'Or is it that your girlfriend's father is beyond suspicion?'

'She's not my girlfriend,' said Hamish hotly. 'I am looking into all aspects of the case, that's all.'

'Get me something concrete on Ionides, and I'll have your search warrant. There's something wrong about you and this case, Hamish. I think your mind's beginning to wander. Not holding out on me, are you?'

'No, no,' lied Hamish, now anxious to get off the phone. 'I'll let you know if there's anything further.'

He sat chewing his knuckles in a sudden fit of nerves. What if he really was clutching at straws? What if Priscilla's father should turn out to be guilty?

There was a knock at the kitchen door. Hamish went to answer it, sure that it would not turn out to be any stranger. They always knocked at the front door.

Josie Darling was standing there when he opened it.

'What is it?' asked Hamish.

'Can I come in?'

He stood back. She hobbled into the kitchen on stiletto heels and sat down in a chair. 'You've been asking people if they remembered anything?'

'Aye.'

'Well, I didn't think much of it cos I was so terrified about everyone finding out about me and Murdo. But there was one little thing.'

'What?'

'I was down on the waterfront . . .'

'When?'

'Two days before Fergus disappeared.'

'And . . .'

'I saw him with Callum McSween.'

'So?'

'He was jeering at Callum and saying he knew Callum would soon be broke, and Fergus was bragging about his new salary and saying that he bet Callum would like some money like that, and Callum said, "Get away from me or I'll break your neck."'

'And you never thought to tell me afore this!'

'Like I said, I was frightened that folks would find out my wedding was off. I remembered and told Mother, and Mother said it was

191

funny Callum hadn't gone for work at the new hotel like a lot of other people because they were paying labourers good money.'

'Thanks, Josie, I'll look into it.'

'Do you think Callum killed Fergus for his job?'

'I doubt it. Callum was recommended by me. But I'll have a word with him. He should have told me about the row with Fergus.'

Hamish saw her out. Then he got into the Land Rover and drove up to Callum's croft.

Callum and his wife were sitting in their kitchen eating steak and chips. The kitchen door was open so Hamish walked in.

'Welcome, Hamish,' said Callum. 'Would you like some food?'

Hamish's stomach gave another rumble. 'No, I'm in a hurry. I've got an appointment.'

'So what brings you? Sit down, man, and take the weight off your feet.'

Hamish removed his peaked cap and sat down.

'Callum, why didn't you tell me you had a row with Fergus?'

Callum looked awkward. 'Care for a dram?'

'No, Callum. What was it about, and why didn't you tell me?'

Callum looked down at the table and pushed his food around his plate with his fork.

'Somehow he'd found out I was in financial trouble, and he knew I'd failed to get a job at the hotel.'

'Wait a bit. You didn't get a job at the new hotel? Why? A lot of it is chust plain labouring.'

'I don't know why. I was interviewed by that Greek.'

'Ionides?'

'Yes, him.'

'Funny, you'd think he'd have a manager or have got that secretary of his to do the hiring.'

'It was himself. And he said he was pleased to be giving work to the locals knowing how we'd all suffered with the drop in the price of sheep.'

'And then?'

'He said he didn't want any of the carpets or furnishings or building materials wandering off. He said he knew us Highlanders had a reputation for theft. I got a wee bit angry. I said I had never taken anything in my life that didn't belong to me. I said if there was one thing I couldn't stand, it wass a crook. I said, furthermore, if I knew of anyone getting up to any crookery, I would report that man to the police.'

'And he said?'

'He said he had other people to see, and he would let me know. I wrote down my name, address and phone number. I neffer heard a word after that. I went to the hotel and that Miss Stathos told me they already had enough employees. Man, I wass sick to my stomach.

When you got me the dustman's job, it seemed like a miracle.'

'Look here, Callum. You should ha' told me this afore.'

'I didn't want to,' Callum mumbled. 'It might look bad for me, me having had words with the man and then him getting murdered. That Fleming woman might have sacked me. Do you need to put in a report, Hamish?'

Hamish buried his head in his hands. He had kept secrets from headquarters before, but never so many. He raised his head. 'I'll let you know, Callum. I'll let you know.'

Hamish then drove to the Tommel Castle Hotel. Priscilla met him at the entrance. 'He's up in my apartment,' she said. 'Follow me.'

Priscilla had an apartment at the top of the hotel. The one concession to modernity the colonel would not make was installing a lift, and so they trudged up the stairs. 'Has he said anything?' asked Hamish.

Priscilla shook her blonde head. 'Not to me. He's waiting for you.'

In her small sitting room, the colonel was waiting, tweedy and defiant. 'I don't know what all the fuss is about,' he growled. 'I thought the man was poaching and gave him a bawling out.' But his eyes shifted away from Hamish's face.

Hamish took a gamble. 'I have to hear it

all from you in your own words. You were overheard.'

The colonel turned red and stared at the floor.

'So you'd better tell me,' said Hamish gently.

The colonel raised his head and became all man-to-man bluff geniality. 'You're a friend of the family, Hamish. There's no need for this to go any further.'

'Tell me.'

'That new hotel,' said the colonel. 'Fergus told me he had proof that they were going to poison my river, take my staff, things like that.'

'What proof?'

'He said he had a fax from someone in London to Ionides.'

'So why did you not come straight to me?'

There was a silence. The colonel stared at his highly polished shoes.

'Come on,' urged Hamish. 'Out with it!'

'He offered to sell me the fax. I told him to get lost. I told him he could rot in hell.'

'But why didn't you come to me with this? And if Fergus had such proof, why didn't he demand money from Ionides to keep quiet?'

'I'm coming to that,' said the colonel sulkily. 'I went straight to see Ionides. Seems a charming chap. He said that Fergus had already been to see him. He said there was no such fax and that Fergus was a fantasist, his brain addled by the drink. He took me on a tour of the hotel and pointed out mine was more a country house place, and, besides, he didn't have the fishing or shooting that I had. He said he was going in for tourists, conventions, coach parties, stuff like that. We got on very well. I mean, who was I going to believe? A reputable hotel owner or a drunken dustman?'

Hamish stared at him, amazed. 'But didn't you think, when Fergus was murdered, that he might be on to something?'

'But I couldn't say anything then,' said the colonel. 'The police would have wondered why I didn't come forward. Also, I didn't think for a minute it could be anything to do with Ionides. Men of his substance don't need to go round bumping off people. I thought it was probably Fergus's wife. Anyway, I decided to sit tight.'

'By sitting tight,' said Hamish wrathfully, 'you may have caused the death of Angus Ettrik.'

'That's a bit far-fetched.'

Hamish clutched his head.

'Look,' he said, 'I'm going to have to put in a full report. I wanted a search warrant for Ionides's office, and you have given me reason to get one.'

'Couldn't you keep it quiet?' pleaded the colonel. 'You'll make me look like an awful fool. I mean, do you think Fergus really had such a fax?'

'Yes, I do, and I wonder what became of it. I'm sorry. I have a whole lot of stuff to tell headquarters in the morning, and a lot of people are going to get hurt.'

The colonel got to his feet and marched to the door. 'Your trouble, Hamish Macbeth,' he said, 'is you have no loyalty.'

When her father had gone out, slamming the door behind him, Priscilla sank down wearily into an armchair and groaned. 'What a mess. Do you really have to report him, Hamish?'

'There's a lot more than your father I have to report, Priscilla.'

'The thing is,' said Priscilla, 'why did Fergus go to Father?'

'That's easy. He tries to blackmail Ionides and is told to get lost. Maybe he finds Ionides a bit frightening. So he tries to get money out of the colonel. He may have taken a copy of the fax. He may have thought he'd hit the jack-pot and that he could get money out of both. The thing that worries me is that I'm pretty damn sure there's not an incriminating piece of paper in that office of his. It's no use getting Callum to search through all the hotel rubbish for papers. After Fergus's approach, they prob-ably learned to burn anything incriminating. Och, what a mess!'

'Who else are you covering up for?'

'Priscilla, I'm that hungry. I'll tell you if you get me some food.'

'Wait there.'

Hamish lay back in the chair and closed his eyes. He was depressed and weary. I'm losing

197

my touch, he thought. Dammit, I'm losing my brains. Where have I got for covering up for people? What if it isn't Ionides? But it's bound to be.

He fell into a light sleep and jerked himself awake when Priscilla came in bearing a tray of sandwiches and a pot of coffee.

'Your policeman is doing wonders in the kitchen. He's a natural. He must be earning a bit as well. Three of the diners have sent him their compliments along with a tip. I've never known that to happen before.'

She sat down and waited until Hamish had wolfed down all the sandwiches.

'So what's been going on?' she asked.

Hamish began at the beginning, telling her all about the letters, all about the blackmail, about how the new schoolteacher had lied.

Priscilla waited until he had finished. He had expected her to call him a fool, forgetting that his lingering resentment at Priscilla often put words into her mouth that she never used.

Then she said calmly, 'I don't really see what else you could do.'

He raised his eyebrows in surprise.

'I mean, think about it, Hamish, you've always managed to succeed by using your intuition rather than your brain.'

Hamish winced.

'You know what I mean. You must have had a gut feeling that no one in this village would kill one of their own. I'm thinking of Angus.

But I see your dilemma. You really can't hold out any longer. But when you get permission for this police search, a whole team will come from Strathbane, and we can leak it to the press. A stink like that will hurt Ionides's trade and might make any of the staff who've decided to leave us think again.'

Hamish's face brightened and then fell. 'But I can't help thinking of poor Mrs McClellan and Mrs Docherty, dragged off to Strathbane to be grilled by Blair.'

'Someone told me he was ill.'

'I'll bet he's back on duty and nastier than ever. That man's got the most resilient kidneys and liver in the world. If he dies and there's ever an autopsy and they take those organs out, they'll be able to bounce them along the floor like rubber balls.'

'We must try to think of something,' said Priscilla.

Despite his worry, Hamish was warmed by that 'we'.

'Somehow,' Priscilla went on, 'we've got to think of a way of finding a bit of proof within the next few hours.'

'It is a self-imposed deadline, Priscilla. I could always put it off for another day.'

'I don't think you can put off Father's bit of proof. I know he'll be in trouble, but Ionides mustn't be allowed to get away with it.'

They sat in silence. If only this case were

solved, thought Hamish. If only we could sit here like in the old days.

Priscilla sat up straight. 'The bottle bank,' she said 'The one with the paper.'

'What about it?'

'I went to Patel's last Sunday to buy the papers, and you know what the Sunday papers are like, full of stuff nobody wants to read, supplement after supplement. They've got as big as American papers. I remember reading once that there was a newspaper strike in New York, and they sold the British papers on the street, and one man lifted a whole pile thinking it must be like *The New York Times*, and the bundle he took must be all the one paper. Anyway, I put the papers in the car and took out all the bits I didn't want to read to put in the bottle bank. There was even an article in one about saving the forests, and yet I had a whole tree's worth to throw away.'

'Where's this leading, Priscilla?'

'The bottle bank was full. It hadn't been emptied.'

'You mean, any stuff from the hotel might have been shoved in there?'

'It's a long shot.' Priscilla sank back in her chair. 'But the bottle bank weighs a ton. How could we ever get the stuff out?'

'Tam Gillespie over at Braikie's got a crane.'

'The phone's over there, Hamish. Let's get started.'

'Won't Ionides smell a rat when he sees all the activity?'

'Someone said he took off in his helicopter. With any luck, he won't be back until morning at the earliest.'

'Right!' Hamish sat down at Priscilla's desk and pulled the phone towards him. He phoned Tam Gillespie. 'Tam, it's Hamish here. It's an emergency. I need you to bring your crane down to Lochdubh to lift up the bottle bank. There's evidence in there that might save some people in the village from a lot of trouble.'

A voice quacked at the other end. Hamish turned to Priscilla. 'He says he can lift it up, but we'll need something to open it at the bottom.'

'A crowbar,' said Priscilla calmly. Hamish turned back to the phone. 'Chust bring the crane along, Tam. We'll do the rest.' He replaced the receiver and then said, 'Now we need searchers.'

'Let's go for broke and get out the whole village,' said Priscilla. 'Move over. I'm going to phone Mrs Wellington.'

'She'll never go for anything illegal like this!'

'She will if I ask her.'

Priscilla changed places with Hamish and dialled the number of the minister's wife. 'Mrs Wellington,' began Priscilla. 'We – that is, Hamish Macbeth and myself – are having the bottle bank with the papers opened up. We need to collect any correspondence to the new hotel for evidence.'

Hamish heard Mrs Wellington's booming voice asking questions. 'If we don't,' said Priscilla when the voice at the other end of the line had finally fallen silent, 'then some of our own could be under suspicion. I feel we all have a God-given duty to help the righteous.' Priscilla winked at Hamish.

Then Hamish heard her say: 'That's very good of you. The fishermen? But they're out at the fishing. Oh, I'll tell Hamish.'

When she rang off, she said, 'We'll need to be quick. The fishermen haven't gone out because there's a storm forecast.'

'Good, let me have the phone, and I'll call Archie and get the men rounded up.'

After Hamish had given Archie instructions, he said, 'I'd better get going.'

'I'm coming with you. Wait till I find a sweater.'

When Priscilla and Hamish drove down into Lochdubh, figures were appearing at doors of cottages. Other figures were making their way along the waterfront towards the bottle bank. It looked as if the whole village was on the move.

They gathered around the bottle bank. Hamish stood up on the seawall beside the bottle bank and said, 'I am looking for any correspondence to do with the new hotel. I need your help to go through everything and give me anything you can find.'

In the faces looking up at him in the star-light, he saw Mrs McClellan, Mrs Docherty and Josie Darling. He had a momentary pang of doubt. But then he steeled himself. It must be Ionides.

They waited in silence. Hamish began to fret. 'Where is that crane?' he asked Priscilla.

'It'll be here soon,' said Priscilla in a com-forting voice. 'Remember, his top speed is probably ten miles an hour.'

Archie Maclean looked up at the starry sky. 'I think that forecast got it wrong,' he grumbled. 'Not even a breath of wind.'

Still they waited. The crowd began to mur-mur and shift restlessly.

Then they could hear the drone of an engine coming over the hills and soon the small crane driven by Tam came into view, its long neck nodding like some prehistoric creature.

Tam jumped down and surveyed the bottle bank. 'It's a big beastie,' he said. 'You break my crane, Hamish, and you'll have to pay for a new one.'

They all waited while Tam started to operate the crane. 'You'll need to reach up and fix the ring o' the bank to the crane.'

Hamish leapt up on the harbour wall again and fixed the hook of the crane on to the ring on the top of the bottle bank. The bell-shaped bank swung up and over. Tam switched off his engine. 'Now what?' he called.

Hamish stood on tiptoe and studied the underside of the bank. 'We need a crowbar.'

'Here,' said Priscilla, handing one up to him. 'I put it in the car before we left.'

Hamish was always amazed at Priscilla's efficiency. 'I'll need something to stand on,' he called, almost as if he expected Priscilla to produce a ladder from her handbag.

'I'll get a ladder,' shouted Archie. They waited until he came back with a metal stepladder. Hamish climbed up. Callum didn't have the necessary tools to release the bottom of the bottle bank. The bank was to be cleared separately by men from Strathbane. He sweated and strained until Geordie Liddell, champion caber tosser, shouted, 'Gie me a try, Hamish.'

Hamish relinquished his place to Geordie.

Geordie climbed up the stepladder, which creaked under his great weight. He gave a gigantic thrust at the crowbar. There was a crack. The bottom of the bank opened and papers hurtled down to the ground.

'Don't rush!' shouted Mrs Wellington, coming forward. 'We'll put all this stuff into bundles, and then we'll all start searching.'

'A bottle of whisky to anyone who finds hotel correspondence,' said Hamish.

They all crowded forward, paying no heed to Mrs Wellington, and began searching. 'Can't see a thing,' someone said. People left for their cottages and returned carrying torches and hurricane lamps. Some women carried a trestle table out from the church hall and other women started laying out cups and cutting sandwiches.

'It's getting like a party,' mourned Hamish to Priscilla.

'Just keep searching,' said Priscilla.

Time passed. After an hour, Hamish looked up at the sky. Black clouds were beginning to stream across the stars, although there was still no wind at ground level.

The papers that had been searched were being laid aside, newspapers, letters, comics, but nothing from the hotel.

'It was a good idea, Priscilla,' groaned Hamish. 'But there's practically nothing left, and now I'm in bad trouble for having wrecked a bottle bank.'

'That bottle bank swung out in an arc,' said Priscilla. 'Maybe some of the stuff went over the harbour wall.'

Hamish thrust his torch in his pocket and vaulted over the harbour wall and down on to the stony shore of the sea loch. He took out his torch and swung it in a wide arc.

Then he saw a large manila envelope lying near the water. He walked to it and picked it up. Holding his torch under his armpit, he opened the envelope. It was stuffed with letters and faxes, headed IONIDES PLC. He sat down on the shingle and began to go through them.

Then he found one from Ionides's London office. 'Dear George,' he read. 'How's the work on the hotel going? I mean, your rival. I know you're mad about fishing, but it's an expensive gamble, and what if them up at the Tommel Castle carry on regardless, even after you've pinched their staff and poisoned their water? Besides, you'll be stuck with two hotels in the back of beyond. Then what about that other business? Are you sure the police aren't sniffing around? To risk so much just for fishing! Anyway, let me know if I can help. Your loving brother, Harry.'

He tucked it carefully into his pocket and read the others. There was a fax. 'Dear Harry. Everything is OK. Don't worry. The police here are morons and the one in this village is subnormal. Come up, soon. Once I get the Tommel Castle, I can restock the river. Love, George.'

'Gotcha!' said Hamish.

He ran to the wall and heaved himself up over the top. 'It's all right, folks,' he called. 'I've got what I wanted.'

'What did you find?' asked Priscilla.

'One incriminating letter. One incriminating fax. I'll have Jimmy and the boys up here in the morning.'

People were yawning and drifting away.

'What about all this paper?' demanded Mrs Wellington.

'We'll see to it in the morning,' said Hamish.

Tam released his crane from the bell bank and then backed off, shouting a warning. The great bell bank fell to the ground with a hollow clang and rolled on its side and then lay there, mouth gaping.

'I'll be down in the morning,' said Priscilla. 'Don't worry about running me home, Hamish. Mrs Wellington says if you want to phone, she'll take me back.'

Hamish nodded and then sprinted for the police station. He phoned Jimmy at home and rapidly described what he had found. 'Grand!' said Jimmy. 'Got the bastard. I'll be along with the men in the morning, and I'll hae a search warrant.'

'I don't think Ionides is back yet.'

'Doesn't matter. We'll get that secretary of his to open up everything.'

'What time will you be here?'

'The earliest I can manage.'

'I'm beat. I'll set the alarm.'

Hamish stretched and yawned. There was a pile of fax paper lying by the machine. He could see it was headed STRATHBANE COUNCIL. That damn woman again. She could wait.

As Hamish slept with Lugs curled against his side and through the wall Clarry, unaware of the drama, slept as well, the wind of

Sutherland rose outside. It hurtled down the waterfront. Paper danced elaborate *entrechats* in the air. Paper stuck to fences and garden walls. Paper hung from lamp standards. And then, as if satisfied with the chaos it had caused, the wind roared away to the east and a quiet dawn rose above Lochdubh.

Mrs Freda Fleming sat at her dressing table in the morning, anxiously surveying her make-up. It was certainly very heavy, but she would look all right on camera. She had tried to contact Hamish Macbeth the day before but had failed to get him. She had then phoned Callum, who had reported that the village looked clean and neat. Anyway, she had faxed Macbeth exact instructions of what was to be expected. She hoped he had found a photogenic child to present the bouquet. It was a pity the London papers had shown no interest, but Grampian television had said they would cover the Greening of Lochdubh. The local papers were coming, and some of the Glasgow newspapers were sending their local men.

She had memorized her speech over and over again. She had been worried about the weather, but it was a beautiful morning.

Hamish was awakened by a ferocious knocking at the door. He opened it and found an excited Jimmy Anderson on the step. 'Come on, Hamish, and see the fun. That secretary, Miss Stathos, is yelling and shouting in Greek.'

'Be with you in a minute.'

Hamish washed and dressed. He went out of the station and then blinked at the mess of paper all over Lochdubh. Well, they could all clear it up later.

Tom Stein groaned as his alarm clock went off. He covered the Highlands for the *Glasgow Morning News*. He had a sour mouth and a blinding hangover, and he remembered he was supposed to get over to Lochdubh and cover some dreary cleanup campaign thought up by that poisonous Fleming woman. He shaved and dressed and then drank two Alka Seltzers, wincing at the noise as the tablets fizzed in the water. In this modern age, he thought bitterly, Alka Seltzer should by now have invented a silent tablet.

He was a middle-aged man with a thin face marred by lines of disappointment. As an elderly actor will take part in yet another crowd scene and dream of glory, so Tom dreamed of having a scoop, having his name on the front of the London papers. But he suffered disappointment after disappointment. Hadn't he sent the first reports of the murder in Lochdubh? But the *Glasgow Morning News* had sent up their own man, and anything he had written had been incorporated into the staff man's story. Tom was a freelancer. He sometimes got a few items in the other papers, but only the *Glasgow Morning News* paid him a retainer.

He drank a cup of black coffee and shuddered. He certainly wasn't going to hit the headlines with this one. There was a knock at the door of his little bungalow, situated in what had once been a respectable suburb of Strathbane but which was going rapidly downhill.

It was his photographer, an equally tired and perpetually disappointed man called Paul Anstruther.

'You ready to go?' asked Paul.

'May as well, but if they publish one line, I'll shoot myself in surprise.'

'Nothing,' said Jimmy in disgust. 'But thanks to you, Hamish, we can charge him with intent to ruin the Tommel Castle. But, man, we cannae charge him with murder.'

A crowd had gathered to watch the police activity. Jimmy had actually arrived at six in the morning. It was now eight and Lochdubh was coming alive.

Josie Darling noticed Geordie Liddell standing at the edge of the crowd in full Highland regalia. She went up to him. 'You off to the Games?'

'Yes,' said Geordie. 'What's going on?'

'Don't know. Will you be tossing the caber?'

'Aye, and throwing the hammer.'

'Is the hammer very heavy?'

'Weighs a ton,' said Geordie. 'I've got it in the Jeep. I'll show you.'

He went to his Jeep and returned swinging the long, heavy, metal hammer. 'Try lifting it, Josie.'

'I can't.' She giggled. 'My, but you're strong!'

Geordie grinned and flexed his muscles under his green velvet jacket. Then he heard Hamish shouting, 'I hear a helicopter.' The crowd fell silent.

'It's so damn early in the morning,' groaned Tom Stein as he and his photographer got into a minibus marked PRESS.

'Are we the only ones?' asked Paul Anstruther.

'Looks like it,' said Tom wearily. 'That biddy Fleming is trying to plead with them to wait for more, but it's just you and me.'

The cavalcade moved off. In the front limousine, Mrs Freda Fleming was doggedly trying to look on the bright side. 'I know that at the moment we only have the representatives from the *Glasgow Morning News*,' she said to the small figure of the provost, who was sitting next to her. 'But mark my words, the others will be making their own way there.'

211

The provost, Mr Jamie Ferguson, shifted uneasily. 'It's an awful lot of money we've been putting out on this. The Labour Party is cracking down on wasteful councils. They'll have something to say about this.'

'It isn't really costing anything,' said Mrs Fleming. 'I mean, I sent the constable full instructions. Lochdubh will bear the expense of the celebrations.'

'If I know Lochdubh,' said the provost gloomily, 'then they'll send us a bill.'

'They can try,' snapped Mrs Fleming. She rapped on the glass. 'Go faster, driver, we're running late.'

'I'm in trouble, Freda,' said the provost. 'The other members of the council want rid of you.'

'They cannot sack me. I am an elected Labour representative.'

'Aye, but they want to give the job of environment officer to someone else.'

'That is ridiculous. To whom?'

'To Jessie Camber.'

'What? That blowsy blonde who goes around flashing her tits? Over my dead body.'

The provost sighed and settled down into an escapist dream in which the murderer of Lochdubh, who everyone knew was still at large, would murder Mrs Freda Fleming. But the dream didn't last very long and reality set in. What on earth had ever possessed him to spend a night with her? She would never let him forget it. He shuddered at the thought of

212

his wife finding out. His wife was remarkably like Mrs Fleming, being well-upholstered and domineering.

In the press bus, the photographer, Paul, was saying to Tom, 'The next time I'm sent on a job like this, I won't even bother to put film in the camera.'

'Come on,' said Tom. 'Something could happen.'

'You're always saying that,' replied Paul. 'You've been saying it for years.'

'Look, there's been two murders in Lochdubh. Maybe we could find out a story.'

'Huh,' snorted Paul. But he checked his camera and, by force of habit, focused it out the window. A dismal-looking sheep stared back.

The crowd on the waterfront at Lochdubh stared up at the helicopter. It came lower. They could clearly see Ionides sitting beside the pilot.

The pilot pointed down.

'They're getting away,' shouted Hamish as the helicopter rose and began to head out over the loch.

'Stand back!' yelled Geordie in a great voice.

He began to swing his long hammer. Round and round he went, faster and faster, the skirts of his kilt swinging out. Then he let go.

The hammer sailed up and towards the helicopter in a great arc. It was a throw that was to be talked about for years to come. The hammer sheered straight through two of the rotary blades on the helicopter.

The helicopter spiralled down over the loch. Hamish could see the sheer terror on Ionides's face as the craft struck the black waters of Lochdubh. The pilot got his door open just before the helicopter struck the water. Ionides seemed trapped in his seat. The last they saw of him he was struggling frantically with the door as the water flooded in.

Hamish pulled off his navy blue police sweater and shirt and dragged off his trousers and unlaced his boots and dived into the loch.

Then Jimmy Anderson could see Hamish struggling with the pilot. 'Help him,' he shouted to his men. But at that moment Hamish rose in the water and punched the pilot full on the chin and then dragged the unconscious body towards the shore, where five policemen ran down to help him.

'What about the other one?' panted Hamish.

'We'll need to get the divers down,' said one.

'What's going on?' shouted Tom as their minibus stopped on the waterfront. Paul darted out of the bus with his camera. He pushed and elbowed his way through people in the crowd, who were staring up at a helicopter. Then he saw them back off as Geordie began to swing his hammer. He clicked and clicked. His heart beat with excitement. Then he took the picture that was to go right round the world as the hammer sailed through the rotary blades of the helicopter.

Behind him, Tom's impeccable shorthand was flying across the pages of his notebook.

Paul was now clicking away at Hamish and the pilot in the loch. He ran down the beach to catch pictures of Hamish landing the unconscious pilot on the beach. As Hamish wearily turned to walk up the beach, in his vest and underpants, Paul, who had moved behind him to get another shot of the pilot, suddenly saw that Hamish had a large hole in the back of his underpants. That photo was to appear on the front of a London tabloid under the heading, ARE WE PAYING OUR POLICE ENOUGH?

Tom ran up to him. 'Get up there,' he shouted. 'Get the Fleming woman's face.'

Screams were sounding along the waterfront. Mrs Freda Fleming was blind to the mayhem that was going on around her. She was staring at the mess that was Lochdubh. Paper was festooned everywhere.

She saw Hamish approaching and ran up to him, screaming, 'You bastard! You did this deliberately!' As Paul gleefully raised his camera, she smacked Hamish Macbeth full across the face. With a reflex action that Hamish was to regret for a long time, he smacked her back, and she burst into noisy sobs.

* * *

215

It was to be a long day. Geordie was under arrest. 'Why?' demanded Hamish furiously. 'All he did was stop a murderer from escaping.'

'Hamish,' said Jimmy patiently, 'we still have no proof that Ionides murdered anyone.'

'I ordered Geordie to throw that hammer,' said Hamish.

'You what?'

'I ordered Geordie to throw that hammer,' lied Hamish stubbornly.

'Man, do you know what you are saying? I'll need to suspend you from your duties, and Blair will have you off the force.'

The two were in police headquarters in Strathbane.

'Get back to your police station,' said Jimmy. 'We're about to grill the Stathos woman, and you'd better pray she cracks and comes up with something.'

Priscilla called round at the police station that evening to find Hamish moodily sitting in his living room with his dog on his lap.

'I did knock,' said Priscilla.

'Sit down,' said Hamish wearily. 'I'm in bad trouble.'

'But you got that pilot, and the divers fished Ionides's corpse out of the water.'

'There's no proof he committed either of the murders. Blair's interviewing the pilot and that secretary. I hope one of them comes up with something. It's the first time in my life I've prayed that Blair is at his nastiest. Then that Fleming woman. God, she lands in the middle of a police operation, and all she can do is scream about the mess of paper in Lochdubh. What's that box?'

'It's my sewing kit. Hamish, television wasn't there but a photographer was. So television news has been showing still photographs of Geordie throwing the hammer, but there was another photograph of you on the beach with your bum hanging out of your underpants.'

Hamish covered his face with his hands. 'What next?'

Priscilla laughed. 'Didn't Mrs Macbeth always tell you to wear decent underwear in case you had an accident? Bring your stuff in and let's go through it.'

'I am not in the mood to haff my underwear examined,' said Hamish huffily.

'Oh, go on. We're not doing anything else. I'm afraid to tell you that Clarry is up at the hotel. I think you've lost a policeman.'

'What does it matter? I've lost my job.'

'What will you do?'

'I don't know. I've got the croft and my sheep.'

'That won't support you, and you'll need to leave the police station. You can stay at the hotel if you like until you figure something out.'

'That's good of you, but I think your father will have something to say about that.'

'He's so relieved you didn't tell the police about him that he'll be happy to let you sleep anywhere. You didn't, did you?'

Hamish shook his head. 'I'm glad I'm popular with someone. Someone's at the door. Could you see who it is and send them away, Priscilla?'

'Right. Wait there.'

He could hear the murmur of Priscilla's voice and then the shutting of the kitchen door. She came back bearing a parcel and a large card. Hamish nudged Lugs off his lap and took the card and parcel. The card had a picture of an improbable Highland scene which looked more like *Brigadoon* than reality. The message simply said, 'To Hamish, from the villagers of Lochdubh.'

Hamish opened up the parcel and found himself looking down at six sets of clean underwear.

'Well, well,' said Priscilla. 'I won't be needing my sewing kit after all!'

Chapter Eight

*Times are changed with him who marries;
there are no more by-path meadows, where
you may innocently linger, but the road lies
long and straight and dusty to the grave.*
                                    – Robert Louis Stevenson

Four weeks had passed since Geordie had
brought down the helicopter, and Hamish was
still suspended. He had spent hours over in
Strathbane being interviewed by a police
inquiry team. Investigations into Ionides's company were still going on. The pilot turned out
to have a long record of violent crime. His last
had been for armed robbery. He had faked an
illness and escaped from the prison hospital. He
was still under arrest, but remained silent.

Geordie, thanks to Hamish sticking to his
story that he had ordered Geordie to bring
down the helicopter, was a free man. His case
had been heard at the sheriff's court in
Strathbane, and Hamish had testified that
Geordie had been only acting on instructions.

219

Hamish had been given a rocket by the sheriff for irresponsible policing.

Clarry had worked out his notice, but was still living at the police station until such time as he considered it decent to move in with Martha.

Hamish fished the blackmailing letters out of the bottom drawer of his desk and decided to put them in the stove. The weather had turned chilly and blustery. He had lit the wood fire in the kitchen and was waiting for the wood to catch before he dropped the letters in when the phone rang.

He put the letters on the kitchen table and went to answer it. It was Jimmy Anderson at the other end of the line, sounding very excited. 'He's broken, Hamish.'

'Who?'

'The pilot, Ian Simpson. He says he wants to do a deal.'

'Oh, aye? And you don't do deals.'

'No, but we promised him a favourable trial.'

'So what has he said?'

'He says that Ionides killed Fergus. He told Fergus he would meet him up on the grazings and pay him ten thousand pounds. He bashed his head in and then got Ian, the pilot, to go back with him in the middle of the night. They wrapped the body in one of the sheets from the hotel. They were going to dump it in the loch when they got as far as the Curries' cottage. Ionides said, 'Let's dump the bastard in that bin. I'm sick of carrying it.'

'And then they did Angus?'

'There's the odd thing. He stubbornly says that Angus never came near Ionides. But he says Ionides was trading drugs. That was the real reason for the hotel so far north. They thought it would be an excellent, quiet landing place. There was a raid on all his hotels during the night and they found drugs in the cellar of the one in Aberfoyle, so they've arrested the brother. Miss Stathos is crying and wailing and sticking to her story that she knew nothing about it. Mind you, she says he was fanatical about fishing, any kind of fishing, and was determined to get the Tommel Castle Hotel. Things look better for you, Hamish. You're to attend a special meeting this afternoon at two o'clock.'

'Another dressing down,' said Hamish.

'Aye, but take my advice, laddie, and look meek and humble.'

After he had rung off, Hamish went into the kitchen and looked thoughtfully at the letters. Surely Ionides had killed Angus. It couldn't be anyone else. But he picked up the package and carried it through to the office and put it back in the drawer.

He brushed and pressed his uniform and wondered what awaited him in Strathbane. He hoped no one had reported that Clarry was still living at the police station or he would be in worse trouble than he already was.

Detective Chief Inspector Blair was a happy man. Hamish Macbeth would be removed from his job. No more would that lanky Highlander plague him. He wished now that he hadn't turned the case over to Jimmy Anderson. But he had been feeling weak and shaky after his last bout of drinking and his subsequent treatment in hospital.

He had been off the booze for six weeks now, and he was feeling fit and well. It all went to show he could take it or leave it. Still, the sacking of Hamish Macbeth demanded some sort of celebration. He went to his usual pub and virtuously ordered a glass of tonic water with ice and a slice of lemon.

Hamish stood in front of a long desk and faced his judges. Superintendent Daviot was there, flanked by two hard-faced investigators from the Internal Investigations Department, the chief constable, and Daviot's secretary, Helen, who looked happy because she disliked Hamish almost as much as Blair did.

They went over all the old ground. Hamish did not have any right to order a citizen to throw a hammer at a helicopter, which had resulted in the death of the owner. Hamish stood and listened, his face impassive.

'I am sorry, Macbeth,' concluded Daviot, 'but there is no alternative but to remove you from the force.'

'Wait a minute,' said one of the detectives, raising his hand. 'The fact that Ionides was a murderer and a drug runner and a scab on the face of society puts a different complexion on the matter, in my opinion. Had it not been for Macbeth here, we would never have got on to him. There is another factor. The pilot swears blind they had nothing to do with the murder of Angus Ettrik. I cannot see he had any reason to lie. He could well have lied and claimed that Ionides was totally responsible for the murder of Fergus.'

'Maybe he didn't mind saying he helped in one murder but did not want to say he had assisted in two,' said Daviot.

'I don't think so. This officer —' the detective pointed a pencil at Hamish — 'has had several remarkable successes in the past. I know you don't like his methods, sir, but nonetheless, I am worried because I think we have an unsolved murder here, and Macbeth knows his territory and the people in it.'

Daviot said, 'Would you wait outside, Macbeth?'

Hamish walked stiffly out, his cap under his arm. He sat down in Helen's chair and swung it to one side and then the other. Then he rose and raided Helen's cupboard, where he knew the biscuits were kept. He made himself a cup of coffee on her machine. She would be furious, but he would probably never have to see her again.

Time passed. His eyes drooped. He fell asleep with his feet on Helen's desk.

When Helen came out after an hour to summon him back, she took in the spectacle of the empty coffee cup – her own private best china coffee cup – the plate full of biscuit crumbs and the sleeping constable. Her face flamed with anger. 'Officer Macbeth!' she shouted in his ear.

Hamish jerked awake. 'Och, it iss yourself, Helen,' he said amiably.

'Get in there!' snarled Helen.

Hamish got lazily to his feet. 'My, your colour is awfy bad, Helen. It could be the high blood pressure.'

He smiled at her and walked past her into the room.

'Macbeth,' said Daviot, 'as a punishment you will lose your sergeant's stripes. But you will continue your duties in Lochdubh. You will see Detective Anderson before you leave, and he will brief you. That will be all.'

Hamish went out, feeling dazed and happy. He still had his job and his beloved police station.

He went down to the detectives' room where he found Jimmy. 'So you're still with us,' said a grinning Jimmy. 'Reduced to the ranks.'

'Aye, but I've still got my job,' said Hamish happily.

Jimmy handed him two enormous folders. 'What's this?'

'You'll need to try to find out who murdered Angus. I'll be over there with Macnab to go over the case with you. In those folders are all the interviews after the death of Angus. Go through them again and see if there's anything there we can work on. Now, off with you. I've got a phone call to make.'

When Hamish had left, Jimmy dialled the number of the pub where he knew Blair to be and asked to speak to him. 'This is a great day, Jimmy,' crowed Blair over the phone.

'That it is,' said Jimmy smoothly. 'We never like to see one of our own get the push.'

There was a shocked silence. Then Blair roared like a bull in pain, 'D'ye mean tae tell me that pillock's still got his job?'

'Yes, but he isn't a sergeant any more.'

'How did he get away with it?'

Jimmy was enjoying himself immensely. 'I don't know. I wasn't there, but they phoned down and asked me to brief him on the Angus Ettrik case.'

Blair uttered a stream of Anglo-Saxon words and then slammed down the receiver. He went back to his table in the bar. He had gone back to the police canteen for his lunch and, because it was his day off, had returned to the pub through force of habit. A nearly full glass of tonic water winked at him in the flashing lights of the fruit machine next to the table. He picked it up and strode to the bar. 'Put a double gin in there,' he shouted. Blair was normally a whisky drinker, but there was no point in wasting good tonic water.

Hamish whistled and sang as he drove back to Lochdubh with Lugs beside him. Once clear of Strathbane, he stopped the Land Rover on a grassy verge and let Lugs out. The animal had been cooped up for too long. As he watched Lugs scampering through the heather beside the road, he had a sudden memory of Kirsty Ettrik's fear when she had seen his dog.

His happiness fled. If Angus had not been murdered by Ionides, then it followed it must have been done by someone in Lochdubh. If Fergus had confided in him about the hotel, might he not have confided in him about the other people he had been blackmailing?

He wondered if Priscilla was back. She had left for London a few days after the death of Ionides. He looked over his shoulder at the two folders. He persuaded himself that he only wanted to see Priscilla again to use her help. She had a logical mind.

He whistled for his dog and then reached over and helped Lugs up on to the high seat. He fastened the seat belt around the dog and then set off again.

Once back at the police station, he fed Lugs and then settled down to pick the sergeant's stripes off his two police sweaters and then his tunic.

Clarry came in and beamed all over his face when Hamish gave him the good news.

'It couldn't have come at a better time,' said Clarry. 'I'm packing up today and moving in with Martha. We're getting married next year. Will you be best man?'

'I'd be delighted, Clarry. How are things going on at the hotel?'

'I've never been happier, Hamish.'

Clarry had slimmed down and was always clean and fresh looking, a big change from the slob of a constable who had first come to Lochdubh.

'The thing is, Clarry,' said Hamish, 'they've reopened the investigation into Angus's murder.'

'That's daft. It was that Greek, surely.'

'They don't think so. The pilot's confessed that Ionides killed Fergus, and he helped to dump the body, but he swears blind that his boss had nothing to do with the murder of Angus.'

'He'd expect leniency for helping solve one murder. If he says Ionides didn't kill him, then he's clear of a more serious charge.'

'That's what I thought. Me and my famous intuition. I ended up concentrating on Ionides, so delighted it wasn't one of us, that of course I thought Angus's murder was done by him.'

'Where'll you start?'

'I've got two big folders of printouts of what everyone interviewed said after Angus's murder. Clarry, gossip to the staff up at the hotel. But keep this under wraps. People at the hotel might gossip a bit more freely if they think the murder solved. People will aye try to protect people, and that's what always stops me getting at the truth.'

Clarry went off to pack his suitcase, and Hamish settled down and began to go through the folders. Kirsty had said that Angus had believed their troubles to be over. What did that mean? Angus's bank account had been checked and there was nothing other than an overdraft.

He phoned up Angela, the doctor's wife. 'Is Kirsty up at the croft?'

'I believe so. I saw her the other day in Patel's. What's this about?'

'I chust wanted a word with her; see if she's all right.'

'Are you all right?'

'Yes, I've still got my job.'

'Come round for a coffee when you can.'

Hamish buttoned on his tunic, minus the three stripes. He called to Clarry, 'I'm going out.'

Clarry appeared in the doorway. 'You've got nothing for your dinner as usual. Call round at the kitchen. I've got some nice braised venison. It'll do you and Lugs a treat.'

'I might do that. Is Priscilla back yet?'

'I heard she might be on her way up.' Clarry drew himself up and said, 'I would just like to say that you were the best boss a man ever had. I will never forget your kindness. Furthermore . . .'

'That's all right,' said Hamish, turning red with embarrassment. 'I'm off.'

'May I give you a hug?'

'Well, no, Clarry. Take care of yourself and stop watching those touchy-feely soaps.'

Hamish drove up to Kirsty's croft house.

She jerked open the door as if she had been waiting, had noticed his arrival.

'How are things, Kirsty?'

'Oh, it's yourself, Hamish. I'm managing as best I can. Everyone around is giving me help with the sheep until I decide what to do. Come in.'

Hamish walked into the kitchen. It sparkled and shone. Every surface gleamed, and the air smelled strongly of disinfectant.

Hamish removed his hat and put it on the kitchen table. 'I don't want to distress you, Kirsty, you've been through a lot.'

Her eyes widened. 'What's happened? Not another death? I mean, it's all over. It was that Greek bastard who killed my Angus.'

'Maybe.'

'What d'ye mean, "maybe"?' she demanded shrilly.

'At Strathbane, they're beginning to think that maybe someone else murdered Angus.'

Her face turned white, and she clutched at the table for support.

'Sit down, Kirsty,' said Hamish, in that moment hating his job. 'There may be nothing in it.'

'But if it's possible there's someone else,' she whispered, 'he could be out there, waiting for me, and I'm up here on my own.'

'There, now. We have to examine everything, and there iss no reason why anyone should come after you.'

'But it was all over,' she wailed. 'After the funeral, I had to try to put my grief behind me.'

Hamish said quietly, 'I'll need to ask you if he said anything at all that might be of help. Now, I know you were in shock right after the murder. But you said that Angus had said your troubles were over. And he had a phone call from the same box on the waterfront that Fergus got his last call from. Now, he was, I

230

gather, fairly friendly with Fergus. Fergus was attempting to blackmail Ionides. He may have told Angus what he had. And after his death, Angus, desperate not to lose his croft, might have tried the same trick.'

'If he did, he said nothing to me,' said Kirsty.

'I cannae myself believe yet it was anyone else. There's that phone call. That's what bothers me.'

'I'm tired of all this.' Kirsty leaned her head on her hand. 'I just want to put it all behind me.'

'I'm asking you, however, to think and think hard,' said Hamish. She stayed where she was, silent, and after a few moments, he let himself out.

He then drove to Elspeth MacRae's croft. 'Come in, Hamish,' she said happily. 'I was just about to have a cup of tea.'

How relaxed everyone was now that they thought the murders were solved. Hamish went into the stone-flagged kitchen. A peat fire burned in the hearth and an old clock ticked noisily on the wall, the chintz curtains fluttered at the open window: a scene of Highland tranquillity, far removed from murder and mayhem.

'It iss not really the social call,' said Hamish awkwardly to Elspeth's back as she busied herself pouring boiling water into a teapot. Her back stiffened. She carefully put the lid on the teapot, placed it on a tray along with two mugs, milk, sugar and biscuits, and carried it to the kitchen table.

'I don't see what it can be,' said Elspeth. 'You have my sheep dip papers. Help yourself to sugar and milk.'

'It's like this,' said Hamish. 'It seems there's a possibility that Angus was murdered by someone else.'

'How can that be?'

'The pilot swears blind that neither he nor Ionides was responsible for that murder. And yet it's strange. For Angus got that call before he went out, and we traced it to that call box on the waterfront.'

She lowered her eyes quickly. Hamish eyed her sharply. 'What iss it? You've got to tell me.'

She clasped her hands and said in a low voice, 'You've known me a long time, Hamish.'

'Yes.'

'You know I'd never hurt a fly.'

'What have you been keeping from me, Elspeth?'

A sheep bleated nearby and a gust of wind blew around the cottage. The clock ticked away, marking out the seconds of her silence.

'Angus was going to sell me his croft house,' she finally said, 'and then, having the house, I was going to apply to the Crofting Commission for the tenancy of the land. He had been saying one day he would do it, then the other that he had changed his mind. I was down in the village, and I saw the phone box and decided to call him before I got home and see if he had come to any decision. He sounded excited, happy, said something had come up. He said he would drive over and tell me. I said I was phoning from the village, and I would see him at my place. I went home and waited and waited. And then I heard he'd been murdered.'

'So why didn't you tell me or any policeman that it wass you that made the call?'

'I was shocked. I didn't know the call was important. I was shocked, Hamish,' she repeated.

Hamish sighed. 'I may need to take a statement from you, Elspeth. You should neffer have held back information like this.'

'But I had nothing to do with the poor man's murder!'

'Someone did. It looks as if it was you he was going out to see. Wait a minute, I remember Kirsty saying he had told her to go away somewhere and leave him for a bit. I mean, why would he do that if he was the one that was going out? I'm sorry, but there's no way I can keep this bit of evidence quiet.'

'Then you can take yourself off,' said Elspeth. 'Just get out of my house. If it's a choice between your friends and the police, you'll always stick to the police. You're a fascist!'

'I'm off,' said Hamish. 'But I want you down at the police station at ten o'clock tomorrow morning.'

As he left, he damned the secretiveness of the locals. What other bits of evidence were some of them keeping from him?

He went back to Kirsty. 'What is this?' she demanded angrily. 'Haven't you upset me enough for one day?'

'Kirsty, you never told me Angus was thinking of selling to Elspeth.'

'Oh, that. He changed his mind from day to day.'

'But Elspeth was the one who phoned him, and he told her he was going to drive over and see her. He sounded happy. He said something had come up.'

'I didn't hear any of that. I'm telling you, he told me to make myself scarce. What did Elspeth phone him about? And why did she call from that box?'

'She happened to be in Lochdubh. Evidently Angus was dithering about selling the house to her.'

'He didn't mean anything by it. He would get frightened by the debt and then say he was going to sell the place, but he could never make up his mind.'

'Kirsty, a lot of people seem to have been holding back bits of information from me that might help. Are you sure there's nothing you're not telling me?'

'What else can I tell you?' demanded Kirsty. 'My husband's been murdered. I've been coming to terms with my loss, and now you tell me the murderer is still out there! Oh, go away and leave me in peace.'

Hamish looked down at her and shuffled his large police boots. 'I'll be off now. But I'll be calling on you again.'

He went back to the Land Rover. 'It was that dog of yours,' Kirsty shouted after him. 'It's brought evil.'

Hamish drove off. He realized with a heavy heart that he would need to do the rounds of the people Fergus had been blackmailing in case Angus had taken up his role.

Josie would be at work in Strathbane, so he headed for the banker's house. Mrs McClellan answered the door to him. How welcoming everyone was now and how much fear he was going to bring back into their lives.

'Come in,' she said. 'I want to thank you so much for keeping that matter quiet. I can sleep at nights now.' He followed her through to the kitchen at the back. 'Take a seat. Coffee?'

'Maybe not now,' said Hamish. 'I've bad news.'

She stood very still.

'It's Angus's murder. It seems there's a good

chance he might have been murdered by someone else.'

She sat down abruptly. 'But you have that cutting?'

'You're safe there, for the moment. I still haven't reported it. You see, Ionides's pilot, he says his boss had nothing to do with Angus's murder, and he's sticking to it. As you've probably read in the papers, it was Ionides who killed Fergus, and the pilot helped him dump the body. But there's still a big question mark hanging over Angus's death.'

'And I'm a suspect?'

'I just have to start going over all the old ground. Did you know Angus?'

'Only by sight. Angus and Kirsty. I saw them at socials at the church, that sort of thing. I knew both of them to say hullo, but never anything more than that.'

'And Angus never approached you after Fergus's death?'

'No.'

He looked at her intently. He was sure she was telling the truth.

'Look, a lot of people in this village know things, but they haven't been telling me because they don't want to get involved with the police, or because they think they're protecting each other. If you can remember anything, or hear anything . . .'

'I'll let you know.'

* * *

Hamish next called on Mrs Docherty. It was the same thing: the warm welcome changing to distress as he explained the reason for his call.

'Do you still have that dreadful letter?'

'I'm afraid I still have it. I can't do anything about it until Angus's murder is cleared up. Have you heard from that man, the travelling salesman?'

'He wrote once more, saying he would be back in Strathbane. I phoned him and told him he had to forget he ever saw me or he would maybe be part of a murder investigation. I haven't heard from him since.'

'And Angus didn't approach you in any way?'

'No, he didn't. But it was a vicious murder. Surely it was done by a man.'

'Any woman with something like a hammer could have done the job.'

She shuddered. 'So there's a murderer out there?'

'Let's just hope that pilot was lying, but I've got to keep trying.'

He waited until evening, when he knew Josie would be home. 'Where's your mother?' he asked as he followed her into the living room.

'Working up at the hotel. She had to beg for her old job back.'

He sat down and told her that the murder of Angus was open again for investigation. Josie stared at him in open-mouthed dismay. 'But what's it got to do with me?'

'It could be that Fergus told Angus who he was blackmailing and Angus might have tried the same thing. He didn't approach you?'

'No.' Although the living room was cold, there was a sheen of sweat on Josie's face. She looked frightened to death. 'It'll all come out again,' she said.

'There's nothing to come out that folks don't know about,' said Hamish. 'Think about it, Josie. You started cancelling the invitations after Fergus was murdered.'

'But Fergus was so pally with Angus. So maybe if someone murdered Angus, they'll come looking for me.'

'That doesn't make sense.'

'But don't you see, there's something about me that can drive men mad.'

Hamish looked at her in comical amazement. Then his eyes sharpened.

'Wait a bit, Josie. You said that Fergus was pally with Angus. How do you know that?'

'I just remembered it was one day last summer, I saw them laughing and chatting down by the harbour.'

'Josie, why didn't you tell me this before?'

'It didn't seem important.'

'If there's any other little thing, you've got to let me know.'

'Sure.' She batted her heavily mascaraed eyelashes at him. 'Would you like a drink?'

'No, thank you. I've got to get going.'

Hamish had a feeling of having escaped from something.

Somewhere in this village, he thought, was someone sitting on an important clue, and they didn't even know it. The whole village of Lochdubh would just need to be interviewed again.

Jimmy Anderson sent three constables over to Lochdubh to help Hamish. They all plodded from house to house until, at the end of a month, there was a large folder of new reports, all containing nothing of any importance at all. 'You'll just need to face up to it, Hamish,' said Jimmy. 'You can't win them all. I thought you were on to something with Elspeth MacRae, but she seems pretty clear apart from withholding information.'

As the dark winter nights settled down over Lochdubh and the mountains turned white with snow, Hamish would sit in the police office at night, making notes, studying what people had said, hoping always to find something important he might have missed.

One afternoon the phone rang. It was Clarry. 'The hotel's closing down for a couple of weeks,' he said cheerfully. 'Priscilla's back.'

Hamish's heart gave a treacherous lurch. 'And Martha and I were just thinking we hadn't seen you for a bit. I asked Priscilla if she'd like to pop round for dinner tonight and she said yes, so I said I would try to get you as well.'

Hamish accepted with delight. When he replaced the receiver, he happily pushed away the reports he had been studying and went to prepare himself for the evening ahead.

When he went out fine snow was whipping down the waterfront. He was dressed in his one good suit, tie and clean white shirt. He decided to drive, and so he put Lugs in the passenger seat and set off.

Priscilla was already there when he arrived. The children gave Lugs a rapturous welcome. How different it all was, thought Hamish, looking around. There were pictures on the walls and the cherry red carpet from Angela on the floor. There was the exotic smell of good cooking coming from the kitchen. Martha had her hair cut in a new short style, which made her look years younger. Hamish flicked a quick glance at Priscilla's hands. No rings.

While Clarry went to get them drinks, Priscilla said, 'I hear you're back investigating the murder. Do you still think Angus was murdered by someone else?'

'I don't know,' said Hamish, taking a glass of whisky from Clarry. 'I questioned everyone in the village all over again, and I can find nothing.'

'What will Kirsty do?' asked Martha. 'She can't go on running that croft single-handed, and with this snow, things are going to be rough for her.'

'The other crofters will help,' said Hamish. 'And I think the bank's probably going easy on the overdraft for the moment. How long are you here for, Priscilla?'

'I'll be here over Christmas. It's the one good thing about being a freelance computer programmer: when a contract finishes, I can take time off.'

'I'd better have another word with your father. Is he home? I've tried several times, but he's always been away.'

'He's here at the moment. Oh, he'll be so furious if all that's dragged up again.'

The conversation then became general, about village affairs. Clarry sat beaming all round, the baby on his knee.

When they were sitting round the dining table, which had to be cleared first of toys and paint books, and eating excellent roast beef, Martha said, 'I might call on Kirsty.'

'I didn't know you were friendly,' said Hamish.

'I wasn't friendly. I mean, when Fergus was alive, I wasn't friendly with anyone. But we had a lot in common.'

'How's that? No, Lugs,' said Hamish severely, as the dog put a paw on his knee. 'You've had your supper.'

'I've got a nice marrow bone for him,' said Clarry, getting to his feet. 'I'll get it for him now, and that'll keep him quiet.'

Hamish turned his attention back to Martha. 'What do you mean, you've got a lot in common?'

'Well, we had, rather.'

'Tell me about it.'

'It was one day, a couple of months before Fergus was murdered, I was down at Patel's. I had a black eye, and people had given up asking me about things like that, because I always said things like I had walked into the door. But Kirsty followed me out and said, "My marks don't show. He's too clever for that."

'I pretended not to know what she meant because being secretive had become a way of life. But she rolled up her sleeves and there was a great burn on her arm. "He did that with the iron," she said. So it might help if I talked to her. Because even though her man is dead, it takes a while to get over things like that. Clarry came up behind me in the kitchen only a month ago, and he raised his arm to get something down from the shelf, and I screamed and threw up my hands to cover my face.'

Hamish slowly laid down his knife and fork. 'Martha, along with everyone else in this village, I've been asking and asking if anyone had any information that might shed light on Angus's murder, and all you did was shake your head.'

'I didn't think,' said Martha nervously. 'I mean, there's a sort of freemasonry among battered wives. You don't talk about it. I mean, she's the victim. What has that to do with murder?'

'I'd better see her in the morning if the snow allows me to get up there.'

Clarry, who had given Lugs the bone, looked anxiously at Martha's strained face. 'Can we talk about something else at the moment, Hamish? I don't like her reminded of the bad times.'

Priscilla promptly weighed in, telling funny stories about awkward guests they had suffered at the hotel. Hamish forced himself to put the case out of his mind and the evening ended pleasantly.

When Priscilla and Hamish walked out, the snow had stopped. 'Will you get home all right?' said Hamish.

'I've got snow tyres on the car,' said the ever-efficient Priscilla. 'I heard the weather forecast.'

'When will I see you?' asked Hamish. His breath came out in the cold air like smoke and hung between them.

'I'll take you for dinner tomorrow night,' said Priscilla. 'The Italian's. Eight o'clock?'

Hamish grinned. 'I'll be there.'

In the morning he checked on his sheep, checked on his hens, and returned to put on his uniform and then went to talk to Kirsty. He opened the kitchen door and found the banker's wife, Fiona McClellan, standing on the doorstep.

'There's something's come up you should know about,' she said.

'Come in. Have the roads been gritted?'

'Yes, as I came along the gritter was going along the waterfront.'

'So what have you got for me?'

'It's only a little thing, and my husband would be furious if he knew I had been discussing bank business.'

'Go on.'

'He never tells me anything about people or their accounts, but I've been thinking and thinking about Angus's murder, and I said last night, "That poor crofter's wife, Kirsty. I gather she's in financial trouble." And he snorted and said, "She could buy and sell us." So I asked him what he meant, and he said, "She's just deposited a cheque for two hundred and fifty thousand pounds."'

'Where did she get that sum of money?' asked Hamish. 'I've got to know.'

'He said her premium bonds had come up. He said she had only a hundred pounds of premium bonds, and we have ten thousand, and yet we never win anything like that.'

'Thank you,' said Hamish. 'I'm glad the poor woman got the money. All her troubles will be over. I don't see what help it can be in this case . . .'

'There's one odd thing.'

'What's that?'

'She's only just banked the cheque. It was sent to her last July.'

Hamish stared at her. 'I'll look into it,' he said slowly. 'Was the cheque made out to her or Angus?'

'To her.'

She clutched his sleeve. 'You musn't let my husband know I told you!'

'It's all right. I'll get her bank account checked. Angus's account was checked after his murder.'

When she had left, Hamish went into the office to phone Jimmy. Then he decided to see it through himself. There might be a perfectly innocent explanation.

The fields around Kirsty's croft house were white and bleak under a lowering sky. As he switched off the engine, the eerie total silence of the countryside surrounded him. No dog barked and no bird sang.

He went almost reluctantly to the door and knocked. There was no reply. He stood there with his head cocked to one side, listening, and then he sniffed the air. He smelled something like cooking stew. Of course, she could have placed a pot of stew or lamb on a low heat before she went out. He stepped back and looked at the cottage. He sensed she was in there, waiting for him to go away.

He stepped back and tried the door handle. The door was not locked. He opened it and went in.

'Kirsty!' he shouted. 'Police! Where are you?'

A pot simmered on the stove. The clock ticked on the wall. He heard a short, shallow breath. There was a battered sofa over to one side. He walked across and leaned over it.

Kirsty was crouched down behind it.

She looked up at him with the eyes of a hunted animal.

'Come out of there, Kirsty,' said Hamish heavily, suddenly knowing the truth. 'Come out, and tell me how you killed Angus.'

She stood up and edged around the sofa. She went and sat down at the kitchen table and put her head in her hands.

Hamish removed his peak cap, laid it carefully on the table as if it were a precious object, and sat down next to her. 'It was the money, wasn't it?'

'Will I go to prison?'

'I'm afraid so. What happened?'

'Did you know he beat me?'

'I chust learned that yesterday.' He took her hand in his. 'Tell me, Kirsty.'

She started to speak in a flat, emotionless voice, as if giving evidence in court. With a flash of intuition, Hamish realized she must have lived in dread of this moment, had rehearsed what she must say.

'We got married when we were both eighteen. Too young. Maybe children might have made a difference. No, that's wrong. I'm glad we didn't have children, seeing the way it worked out. The work on the croft got harder. Every time he made some money from the sheep at the sales, he would start out on another idea. First it was the goats. Well, they kept breaking out, and they are very destructive animals. He sold them at a loss. Then it was the deer. But he wouldn't build a proper deer fence, so the beasts just disappeared one night.

'Like all Highlanders, he liked his dram, but it got more and more. The first time he hit me, he was that remorseful after, I thought he would never raise his hand to me again. But he did, over and over. He liked Fergus because Fergus was a drunk, and Angus had become one, too.'

'He didn't have a reputation of being one,' said Hamish.

'Oh, he would never get drunk in the village. He would sit in the evenings, drinking

247

steadily, and watching me, watching me, enjoying my fear. He never knew about that hundred pounds worth of premium bonds. I kept them hidden. I dreamed of winning. I thought if we had money, everything would be all right.

'Then I won. And the cheque arrived. Like a fool I told him. It was immediately his money. He said he'd take it down to the bank and put it in our joint account. He said he was tired of the rough weather in Sutherland, and we would buy a nice farm down in Perthshire, and I saw that he would spend all the money on this farm, he would mismanage it, and the beating would go on. He had been putting up a shelf in the kitchen. The phone rang and he went to answer it. While he was on the phone, I picked up the hammer and hefted it in my hand. I can't say for sure what happened immediately after that, but he came back and sat down and picked up the cheque and said, "Get my coat. I'm off to the bank."

'I snatched the cheque out of his hands and said, "It's mine." He swung round and his face was mad with fury. Then he turned back and stared straight ahead and said, "Give me that cheque, or you know what'll happen to you."

'Everything went blank, and when I came out of it, I was standing there with the bloody hammer in my hand, and he was lying dead on the floor. I took the cheque and hid it up in the rafters. Then I cleaned every surface. I'd forgotten that they'd expect to find my finger-prints everywhere, this being my home. I took a cloth and swept the floor towards the door. Then I went out and stuffed the cloth some-where. I can't remember. Then I went in and phoned and then took his bloody head in my hands and waited. I felt nothing. It was only after that the horror came.'

'What about the whisky bottle on the table and the two glasses?'

'I did that. I wanted it to look as if he was expecting someone from outside.'

Hamish released her hand and took out his mobile phone, called Strathbane and requested escort for a prisoner, giving them the address and directions.

'Did Angus ever hit you so hard you had to go to the doctor?'

'Yes, he broke two of my ribs one night. He was clever. He never hit me where it would show. I went to Dr Brodie, who sent me to hospital.'

'What did you tell Dr Brodie?'

'I said I had fallen.'

'And he believed you?'

'No. I had been to him the year before with a broken arm. I said I must be accident prone. But he was looking at the bruises on my arms. He said, "You'd better stop lying and report that husband of yours to the police."'

'So why didn't you?'

'It had been going on so long ... so long. I kept making excuses for him. I couldn't begin to think how to manage on my own. I felt lost.' She began to cry in a dreary, helpless way. Angus Ettrik, thought Hamish, if you were alive today, I might be tempted to kill you myself.

He rose and took the pot off the stove and put on the kettle. He went into the bedroom to get Kirsty's coat. Two suitcases were lying packed on the bed. She must have been planning to go away somewhere.

He picked up her wool coat and walked back into the kitchen and placed it on a chair. He waited until the kettle had boiled and made a pot of tea. He put a mug of hot, sweet tea in front of Kirsty and handed her a clean handkerchief. 'Drink that,' he ordered. 'You'll need a good lawyer, Kirsty. You can afford it now.'

'Won't they freeze my money?'

'The money's yours. You didn't get it as the result of a crime. Do you want me to get you a good lawyer?'

She nodded. He took out his phone and dialled a number in Inverness. He outlined the case rapidly and told the lawyer to make all haste to police headquarters in Strathbane.

Then he waited and waited. The snow started to fall gently, great white lacy flakes. At last, he heard the sound of the police siren.

When the police arrived, he turned and charged Kirsty Ettrik with the murder of her husband, Angus. He waited until she was led to the police car. He watched until the flashing blue light disappeared into the snow.

With a heavy heart, he got into the police Land Rover and drove back to Lochdubh.

Epilogue

Lord, Lord, how this world is given to lying!
— William Shakespeare

It was once more a sunny summer's day in Lochdubh. Hamish Macbeth and Detective Jimmy Anderson sat out in deck chairs in the police station front garden. The sky above was as blue as the eyes that shone in Jimmy's foxy face. Hamish often marvelled that a man who drank so much could remain looking so fit and healthy.

'So she got off,' marvelled Jimmy again. 'I couldnae believe it. Kirsty Ettrik got off! Mind you, it was thanks to about every villager here going down to the High Court and swearing blind that she had been tormented and beaten near to death by that husband of hers. Took the shine out of your case, Hamish. Daviot wonders how you could have possibly not known what was going on when everyone else in the village did.'

'I can be a bit stupid,' said Hamish, preferring to forget that he had organized the lying himself. He felt a bit guilty. He had hoped that his work for Kirsty would have got her a lighter sentence. He had not expected her to walk free.

'Still, that's another case cleared up. Nothing else happening?'

'Nothing, I'm glad to say. Been as quiet as the grave here.'

'What happens to that hotel at the harbour?'

'Still bound up in red tape, so it sits there, rotting again. Peter McLeigh, who used to own the bar, managed to buy it back, however he did it, so the locals have someplace to go again. Man, you should see it. I thought he would smarten it up. Ionides had all the dirty old tables and fruit machines and stuff cleared out. He was going to make it into a gift shop. But Peter's put everything back the way it was, even the dirt. It looks as dreary as ever.'

'It's Calvinism,' said Jimmy lazily. 'They think drinking in dreary surroundings is appropriate. So where's Kirsty now?'

'Back at the croft house. She'll probably sell out to her neighbour, Elspeth MacRae, and move on.'

'I would have thought she would have wanted to stay, considering the way everyone stood up for her.'

Hamish did not reply. He knew the villagers felt she had deserved some kind of punishment. They would not be too friendly towards her, to say the least.

Jimmy reached down and picked a whisky bottle off the grass at his feet and poured himself another generous measure.

'How's that new schoolteacher getting on?'

'She's left. Funny thing. I thought she was a really sensible woman. She runs about the village, all excitement, and tells everyone she's got a job at Eton. I thought, that's funny, I thought they'd mostly be masters there. So after she left, I phoned Eton College.'

'And they hadn't heard of her?'

'Exactly. The woman's a raving fantasist. She was friendly with the banker's wife, who then tells me the woman was always a compulsive liar. I'm telling you, Jimmy, the things that people in this village knew that they didn't bother to tell me!'

'And what about your love life?'

'What love life?' said Hamish. With all the drama of the arrest of Kirsty, he had forgotten about that dinner date. And then Priscilla had received another contract job, in Milton Keynes this time, and had taken herself off.

'And how's your ex-copper?'

'Clarry is the happiest man you've ever seen. He's got famous chefs checking in at the Tommel Castle to try to find out his secrets.'

'That's grand. Oh, by the way, that Fleming woman lost her job as environment officer, and not only that, she didn't get elected again at the last council elections. She was beaten by a wee lassie from the Green Party, would you believe it?'

'Horrible woman. I've a funny feeling I haven't heard the last of her.'

Jimmy drained his glass and stood up. 'I'd best get going. I'll give your love to Blair.'

'Aye, you do that.'

Hamish went indoors and fed Lugs and then took the dog for a walk along the waterfront. Everything seemed placid and blue. Even the normally black waters of the sea loch reflected the blue sky. A yacht sailed lazily past, heading out to the open sea. The sound of a jazz tune being played on a radio drifted across the water. He leaned on the old stone wall and breathed in the fresh, sunny air.

Two tourists, a middle-aged couple, were standing a little way away from him. He judged them to be tourists and probably American because they wore sensible summer clothes and shoes, whereas the locals wore pretty much the same clothes as they wore all year round, being used to the very short summers and very, very long winters. He heard the woman say in a voice with a Midwest twang, 'Isn't it just perfect? I would love to live in a place like this.' And the man answered with a smile, 'Everything's possible. I wonder what the house prices are like around here.'

Hamish sighed. People who came on the sunny days were often seduced by the sheer beauty of the place. They enthusiastically decided to move house, but, faced with the ferocious winds and the almost perpetual night of winter, they soon sold up and moved on.

'Afternoon, Hamish. You smell of whisky.'

Hamish turned round and saw Angela Brodie, the doctor's wife, standing next to him.

'I just had the one. Jimmy came calling.'

'What do you think about Kirsty?'

'I'm a bit taken aback, to tell the truth. She *did* kill her husband. I expected some sort of sentence.'

'Well, she's back now. Some of us went up to see if she needed anything, but she said she was just fine and didn't even invite us in. What a lovely day!'

'Aye, it is that. When you look around, it's hard to think that anything violent ever happened here. I thought Kirsty would have been selling her story to the newspapers. Her lawyer's fees must have taken most of what she got.'

A sudden shadow swept over them. Angela looked up at the sky. 'Look at that cloud covering the sun. Where did it come from? The sky was as clear as anything a minute ago.'

Lugs suddenly let out a long, wild howl.

Hamish crouched down by his dog. 'What's the matter, Lugs?'

Lugs threw back his shaggy head with the big peculiar ears and let out an even louder howl. Villagers began to gather around. 'Take the beast tae the vet,' said Archie Maclean. 'He's probably eaten something that's hurt him.'

'It's a death, that's what it is.' Jessie Currie's voice.

Hamish scooped the still howling dog into his arms. 'I'll take him home first and see if I can calm him down.'

The dog was shaking and howling as Hamish carried him into the police station. And then suddenly he went quiet and licked Hamish's nose, almost apologetically.

Hamish set him down. Lugs wagged his tail and went to his water bowl.

He stood for a long moment, looking down at his dog, and then suddenly he was off and running to the Land Rover.

I'm being daft, he told himself. But he put on the siren and accelerated out of the village, not stopping until he skidded to a halt in front of Kirsty Ettrik's cottage.

The door was standing open. He ran up to it and inside the house, shouting, 'Kirsty!'

Then he stopped short. Dangling from a hook on a beam in the kitchen was the lifeless body of Kirsty Ettrik. A kitchen chair lay on the floor where she had kicked it over.

He took another chair and stood up on it and forced himself to feel for a pulse. The body was still warm, but there was no life there. He took out a pocket knife and cut the body down

and laid it on the floor. He went into the bedroom and got a sheet and covered those awful,
bulging, staring eyes. There was an envelope
on the table addressed to Elspeth MacRae, and
an open sheet of A4 paper on which Kirsty had
written, 'I can't live with myself any more.'

Hamish backed away to the door and took
out his phone and called Strathbane.

Then he sat down in the sunshine outside
to wait. He could not bear to go back inside
the house.

By evening, Kirsty's body had been removed,
Hamish had typed up his statement in the
police station and sent it to Strathbane. In the
letter to Elspeth, Kirsty had left the croft house
to her.

Lugs came in and put a paw on Hamish's
knee.

'Who are you?' asked Hamish, looking
down at the dog. Then he shook his head as if
to clear the nonsense out of it. Some of the
locals still believed that the dead came back as
seals. He was getting as nutty as they were.

But he sat there a long time, thinking of the
hell that had been Kirsty's life.

'What a waste,' he muttered. 'What a waste.'

A voice called from the kitchen. 'Anybody
home?'

Priscilla!

He leapt to his feet and went through to find her standing there, smiling at him.

She was wearing an impeccably tailored trouser suit, and not one hair on her blonde head was out of place.

'I thought you were in Milton Keynes.'

'That job's finished. Care for that dinner we never got around to?'

Only for a moment did he hesitate. Only for a moment did his mind warn him against opening up old wounds. Who was it who had said, 'There are no new wounds. Only old wounds reopened'?

But every minute of life was surely for living, for any enjoyment one could get. Seize the moment.

'Be with you in a minute,' said Hamish Macbeth. 'I'll just change out of my uniform.'

If you enjoyed *Death of a Dustman*, read on for
the first chapter of the next book in the *Hamish
Macbeth* series . . .

DEATH of a
CELEBRITY

Chapter One

The fault, dear Brutus, lies not in our stars,
But in ourselves, that we are underlings.
                                    – William Shakespeare

Hamish Macbeth did not like change, although this was something he would not even admit to himself, preferring to think of himself as a go-ahead, modern man.

But the time-warp that was the village of Lochdubh in northwest Scotland suited him very well. As the village policeman, he knew everyone. He enjoyed strolling through the village or driving around the heathery hills, dropping in here and there for a chat and a cup of tea.

The access to Lochdubh was by a single, twisting, single-track road. It nestled at the foot of two huge mountains and faced a long sea loch down which Atlantic winds brought mercurial changes of weather. Apart from a few tourists in the summer months, strangers were few and far between. The days went on much as they had done for the past century, although sheep prices had dropped like a stone and the small farmers and crofters were feeling the pinch. From faraway Glasgow and Edinburgh, authoritative voices suggested the crofters diversify, but the land was hard and stony, and fit only for raising sheep.

So Hamish felt the intrusion into his world of a newspaper office was unsettling. The owner/editor, Sam Wills, had taken over an old Victorian boarding house on the waterfront and, with the help of a grant from the Highlands and Islands Commission, had started a weekly newspaper called *Highland Times*. It was an almost immediate success, rising to a circulation of nearly one thousand – and that was a success in the sparsely populated area of the Highlands – not because of its news coverage but because of its columns of gossip, its cookery recipes, and above all, its horoscope. The horoscope was written by Elspeth Grant and was amazingly detailed. Startled Highlanders read that, for example, they would suffer from back pains at precisely eight o'clock on a Monday morning, and as back pain was a favourite excuse for not going to work, people said it was amazing how accurate the predictions were.

But Hamish's initial disapproval began to fade although he thought astrology a lot of hocus-pocus. There were only three on the editorial side: Sam, and Elspeth, and one old drunken reporter who somehow wrote the whole of the six-page tabloid-sized paper among them.

He did not know that the larger world of the media was about to burst in on his quiet world.

Over in Strathbane, the television station, Strathbane Television, was in trouble. It had been chugging along, showing mostly reruns of old American sitcoms and a few cheaply produced local shows. They had just been threatened with losing their licence unless they became more innovative.

The scene in the boardroom was fraught with tension and worry. Despite the No Smoking signs, the air was thick with cigarette smoke. 'What we need,' said the head of television features, Rory MacBain, 'is a hard-hitting programme.' Over his head and slightly behind him, a television screen flickered showing a rerun of *Mr. Ed*. 'People come to the Highlands but they do not stay. Why?'

'That's easy,' said the managing director, Callum Bissett. 'The weather's foul and it's damn hard to make a living.'

As a babble of voices broke out complaining and explaining, Rory leaned back in his chair and remembered an interesting evening he'd had in Edinburgh with a BBC researcher. He had met her at the annual television awards at the Edinburgh Festival. He had been amazed that someone so go-ahead and with such stunning, blonde good looks should be only a researcher. He had been even more amazed when she had taken him to bed. He had promised her that if there was ever any chance of giving her a break, he would remember her.

He hunched forward and cut through the voices. 'I have an idea.'

They all looked at him hopefully.

'Our biggest failure,' he said in measured tones, 'is the *Countryside* programme.'

Felicity Pearson, who produced it, let out a squawk of protest.

'The ratings are lousy, Felicity,' said Rory brutally. 'For a start, it's all in Gaelic. Secondly, you have a lot of old fogies sitting at a desk pontificating. We should start a new series, call it, say, *Highland Life*, and get someone hard-hitting and glamorous to present it. Start off by exploding this myth of the poor crofter.'

'They *are* poor now,' protested Felicity. 'Sheep prices are dreadful.'

Rory went on as if she had not spoken. He said that although people did not like to live in the Highlands, they liked to see programmes about the area. With a glamorous presenter, with a good, hard, punchy line, they could make people sit up and take notice, and the more Rory remembered the blonde charms of the researcher – what was her name? Crystal French, that was it – the more

266

convincing he became. At last his idea was adopted. He retreated to his office and searched through his records until he found Crystal's Edinburgh phone number.

After he had finished talking, Crystal put down the phone, her heart beating hard. This was the big break and she meant to make the most of it. She would be glad to get out of Edinburgh, glad to get away from being a mere researcher. Researchers worked incredibly long hours and had to kowtow to the whims of every presenter. Who would have thought that a one-night stand with that fat little man would have paid such dividends? And she had just been coming around to the idea that a woman can't really sleep her way to the top! She did not realize that her past failure to move on had been because of her reputation for doing just that thing. There were a lot of women executives in broadcasting these days who had got to the top with hard work and brains and did not look kindly on any of their sisters who were still trying the old-fashioned methods, so when her name had come up for promotion there had always been some woman on the board who would make sure it was turned down flat.

Rory, when he met her at the Strathbane Station, was struck anew by her looks. Her long blonde hair floated about her shoulders, and her slim figure was clothed in a business suit, but with a short skirt to show off the beauty of her excellent legs. Her eyes were very large and green, almost hypnotic. Crystal kissed him warmly. She had no intention of going to bed with him again. He had done his bit. He was only head of features. If necessary, she would seduce one of his superiors.

Hamish Macbeth did not watch much television. But he did read newspapers. He was intrigued to read that a new show called *Highland Life* was to start off with an investigation into village shops in the Highlands. He decided to watch it. He expected it to be a series of cosy interviews.

The show was to go out at ten o'clock that evening. He was about to settle down to watch it when there was a knock at the kitchen door. He opened it to find with dismay that he was being subjected to a visit from the Currie sisters. It had started to rain, and the sisters, who were twins, stood there with raindrops glistening on their identical plastic rain hats, identical glasses, and identical raincoats. 'Our telly's on the blink,' said Nessie, pushing past him. Jessie followed, taking off her plastic hat and shaking raindrops over the kitchen floor. 'I was just going to bed,' lied Hamish, but they hung up their coats and trotted off into his living room as if he had not spoken.

Hamish sighed and followed them. The Currie sisters were unmarried, middle-aged ladies who ruled the parish. Jessie had an irritating habit of repeating everything. 'We're here to see that new show, that new show,' she said, switching on the television set. 'Don't you have the remote control, the remote control?'

'I need the exercise,' said Hamish crossly.

'A cup of tea would be grand,' said Nessie.

'I'll get tea during the ads,' snapped Hamish.

'Shhh,' admonished Nessie. 'It's on.'

The presenter was walking down a village street. 'That's Braikie,' hissed Nessie, recognizing a nearby village. Crystal's well-modulated voice could be heard saying, 'People deplore the decline of the village shops. The thing to ask yourself is, would you shop in one? Or do you drive to the nearest large town or supermarket? If you do, what are you missing?'

'That's old Mrs Maggie Harrison's shop she's going into, going into,' said Jessie. 'Oh, look at Mrs Harrison's face. It hasnae been rehearsed, rehearsed. She's fair dumfounert.'

'We're here from Strathbane Television,' Crystal was saying, 'and we are just going to have a look on your shelves.' She picked up a basket. 'That skirt is hardly covering her bum,' exclaimed Nessie.

'What have we here?' Crystal held up a tin of beans. 'Why are so many of these cans bashed?' she asked. She winked saucily at the camera. 'I don't think there is one unmarked tin in this shop.'

'It's because she gets them cheap,' muttered Nessie. 'But she sells them cheap. They're fine. How else is the poor old biddy going to compete with the supermarkets?'

'And this?' A packet of biscuits. 'This is past it's sell-by date.'

And so on and on Crystal went, seemingly oblivious to the fact that Mrs Harrison was trembling and crying.

Hamish felt great relief when this horrible blonde stopped the torment, but it turned out she had moved to Jock Kennedy's general store in Drim, and Jock Kennedy was having nothing to do with her disparaging remarks. 'Get the hell out o' here, you nasty cow,' he roared. And so it went on, from shop to shop.

'So you see,' said Crystal, summing up against a tremendous background of mountains and heather, 'the decline of the village shop is because they cannot possibly offer the same goods at the same prices as the supermarket. Why mourn their passing? Good riddance to bad rubbish, is what I say.'

The Currie sisters sat stunned. 'Well, I never, I never,' said Jessie.

'There's one good thing,' said her sister,

'there'll be so many complaints that the show will be taken off.'

Hamish privately thought that the show would get the response it had set out to get. Infuriated viewers would tune in the following week just to see how nasty it could get, and ratings would soar. There had been very few advertisements, but they would get more.

He switched off the television set and saw the Currie sisters on their way. They were too upset to notice that he had not given them any tea.

Viewers and locals, moved by the humiliation of Mrs Harrison, flooded into her shop during the following week to buy goods and commiserate with her. Newspapers interviewed her. Elspeth wrote a savage critique of the show and a flattering article about Mrs Harrison and her shop. The Highlands were rallying behind the underdog and forgetting that Mrs Harrison sold some quite dreadful goods and that her local nickname had been, before her appearance on television, Salmonella Maggie. Despite Elspeth's writing a further article telling people not to watch the next show because low ratings were the only thing that would get it taken off, everyone in Lochdubh, and that included Hamish Macbeth, switched on for the next airing of *Highland Life*. This episode was called 'The Myth of the Poor Crofter'.

Her first interview was with The Laird. The Laird was not a laird at all, but a crofter called Barry McSween, who had earned his nickname by farming several crofts, so instead of having a croft, which is really a small holding, he had quite a good-sized farm. But the drop in sheep prices had crippled him and his temper had suffered. Sheep were expensive to slaughter because, according to government regulations, the spine had to be removed and that added tremendously to the cost. Hoping that things would get better, he had bought himself a new Volvo, and the camera focused on its new licence plate and gleaming glory before moving in on his red, round face.

At first Crystal wooed him, cooing that things were bad and how was he surviving? Barry, like a lot of people, had privately nursed dreams of being on television. He invited her into his croft house, which in the palmy days had been extended. The camera panned over the expensively furnished living room and then into the large airy kitchen, which had every labour-saving device. Happily Barry bragged about his possessions while Crystal smiled at him and led him on. Elated, Barry preened and volunteered that he had a good voice and would she like a song? Crystal would. Hamish prayed that the unwitting Barry would sing a Scottish song, but he sang 'I Did It My Way', in an awful nasal drone during which the camera moved to Crystal's beautiful face, which was alight with mocking laughter.

When he had finished and was sprawling back in his leather sofa with a smug grin on his face, Crystal started to go in for the kill. She said that in the south particularly, people heard a lot about the poor crofter and were not aware that someone like Barry owned so much land and lived in such luxury. Too late did Barry realize the way the interview was going. He blustered about how he could hardly make ends meet. Crystal went remorselessly on. Barry ended up by ordering her out of his house. It was unfortunate that just at that moment, Barry's wife, who had been ordered to stay away because he wanted the show to himself, should come driving up in her Jaguar. It was an old Jaguar and Barry had got it cheap. But his wife kept it gleaming and well-cared-for and it looked extremely rich.

Had Crystal left it at that, the reaction to her programme might not have been so violent, because Barry was not popular, but she picked on another crofter, Johnny Liddesdale, a quiet little man. The extension to his croft house he had built himself over the years. The furniture inside he had made himself. He stammered and blushed during the interview while Crystal made him look like a fool, and a lying fool at that. How could he plead poverty when he had such a beautiful home? Hamish could

273

not bear to watch any more and switched off the set.

Half an hour later, there was a knock at the kitchen door. The locals never came round to the front of the police station. He opened it and recognized Elspeth Grant.

'Come in,' said Hamish. 'What brings you? Stars foreboding something or other?'

'As a matter of fact they are,' said Elspeth calmly. It was early autumn and the nights were already frosty. She was wearing a tweed fishing hat and a man's anorak. She removed her hat and put her coat over the back of a chair. She had a thick head of frizzy brown hair and sallow skin, gypsy skin, thought Hamish, but it was her eyes that were remarkable. They were light grey, almost silver, sometimes like clear water in a brook, sometimes like quartz, and emotions and thought flitted across those large eyes like cloud shadows over the hills on a summer's day. Her soft voice had a Highland lilt. Hamish disapproved of her. He thought her astrological predictions were making clever fun of the readers.

'Coffee?' asked Hamish.

'Please.'

'It isn't decaff.'

'That's all right. Did you think I would mind?'

'Yes, I thought you were probably a vegetarian as well.'

She leaned her pointed chin on her hands and surveyed him. 'Why?'

'Oh, astrology and all that.' He filled two mugs from the kettle that he kept simmering on top of the wood-burning stove.

'You are a very conventional man, I think.'

Hamish gave her a mug of coffee and sat down opposite her. 'Did you come round here at this time o' night to give me my character?'

'No. Did you see that programme?'

'The one with Crystal French?'

'That's the one.'

'What about it?'

'Someone's going to kill her,' said Elspeth calmly.

'Whit! Havers, lassie. Her nasty programme will run one series. Then there'll be another and the novelty will hae worn off and she'll either sink without a trace or go to London.'

'I don't think so. I think she'll be killed.'

'See it in the stars?' mocked Hamish.

'You could say that. It's something about her. She's *asking* to be killed.'

'And who's going to do it?'

'Ah, if I knew that, maybe I could stop it.'

'I am afraid in the world of television, the wicked can flourish like the green bay tree,' said Hamish.

'Quoting the Bible, Hamish? You?'

'Why not? I am not the heathen. Let's see, you have come here late at night to tell me you haff a feeling.' Hamish's Highland accent always became more pronounced when he was upset. 'And yet you seem a sensible girl. I don't trust you. I think you came along here to have a private laugh at my expense.'

And although Elspeth's face was calm, Hamish had a feeling that somewhere inside her was a private Elspeth who found him a bit of a joke.

She drank her coffee. Then she put on her hat and swung her anorak around her shoulders. 'Don't say I didn't warn you,' she said.

He leaned back in his chair and looked up at her. 'And just what wass I supposed to do about this warning? Phone up my superiors and say I have a *feeling* her life's in danger?'

'You could say you had received anonymous calls from people threatening to kill her.'

'Oh, I should think those sort of calls are already arriving at Strathbane Television.'

She gave a little shrug. 'Well, I tried.'

And then she was gone. She left so quickly and lightly that it seemed to Hamish that one minute she was there, and in the next, she had disappeared, leaving the door ajar.

He tried to dismiss the whole business from his head, but he felt uneasy.

Rory MacBain was basking in Crystal's success. The first two programmes were to run on national TV followed by the subsequent ones. The switchboard had been jammed with angry calls. The mail bag was full of threatening letters. And that *was* success. Reaction was success. He was disappointed that Crystal kept rejecting his advances, but the praise he was receiving for having thought up the idea more than compensated for any disappointment.

There would be more money, much more money for the next series. This one had been thought up on the hoof, with less than a week from the idea to the filming. On Monday, the topic was decided. 'Behind the Lace Curtains' was to be an exposé of what really went on in Highland villages. Researchers burrowed through old cuttings, digging up scandals that people had hoped were long forgotten.

Crystal, who had little to do, as the research was all done for her and scripts written for her, although she preferred to put her own comments into them at the last minute, decided to head out from Strathbane and cruise round various villages. Her path was about to cross that of Hamish Macbeth and on the very day he felt his world had come to an end.

Yesterday morning, he had read his horoscope, Libra, in which Elspeth had written, 'You will receive news on Monday which will make you feel your heart has been broken. But remember, no pain, no gain. This is not the end. This is the beginning of a whole new chapter.'

'Rubbish,' muttered Hamish. He fed his dog, Lugs, and was just getting ready to go out when the phone rang. It was Mrs Wellington, the minister's wife. 'I don't suppose you know,' she said. 'Do you read the *Times*?'

'No,' said Hamish.

'I thought not. It was in the social column four days ago and it's all round the village. I said someone's got to tell Hamish, but then I decided that, as usual, it would have to be me.'

'Tell me what?' asked Hamish patiently.

'Priscilla Halburton-Smythe is getting married . . . Are you there?'

'Yes.'

'It was in the social column. She's marrying someone called Peter Partridge.'

'Thank you.' Bleakly.

Hamish put down the receiver and sat staring blindly at the desk. Lugs whimpered and put a large paw on his knee. Priscilla Halburton-Smythe, daughter of the colonel who owned the Tommel Castle Hotel, had at one time been the love of his life. They had even been engaged. She might have told him. He told himself that he had got over her long ago, but he still felt sad and bereft.

He remembered his horoscope and suddenly got angry. Elspeth would have heard the gossip, Elspeth heard all the gossip. She must have found out the date of his birthday. She must have found it very amusing.

He patted Lugs on the head and said, 'Stay, boy.' He would go out on his rounds as usual, he would work as usual. Life would go on.

He was just getting into his police Land Rover when a bright green BMW did a U-turn on the harbour and raced along the waterfront, well over the speed limit. He jumped in the Land Rover and with siren blaring and blue light flashing, and holding the speed camera gun, that was fortunately on the front seat, out of the window with one hand, trained on the fleeing car, he set off in pursuit.

The BMW stopped abruptly on the hump-backed bridge that led out of Lochdubh. Hamish stopped behind it and climbed down. He leaned down and looked into the BMW and Crystal French looked back.

To order your copies of other books in the Hamish Macbeth series simply contact The Book Service (TBS) by phone, email or by post. Alternatively visit our website at www.constablerobinson.com.

No. of copies	Title	RRP	Total
	Death of a Gossip	£6.99	
	Death of a Cad	£6.99	
	Death of an Outsider	£6.99	
	Death of a Perfect Wife	£6.99	
	Death of a Hussy	£6.99	
	Death of a Snob	£6.99	
	Death of a Prankster	£6.99	
	Death of a Glutton	£6.99	
	Death of a Travelling Man	£6.99	
	Death of a Charming Man	£6.99	
	Death of a Gentle Lady	£6.99	
	Death of a Nag	£6.99	
	Death of an Macho Man	£6.99	
	Death of a Dentist	£6.99	
	Death of a Scriptwriter	£6.99	
	Death of an Addict	£6.99	

And the following titles available from autumn 2009 . . .

No. of copies	Title	Release Date	RRP	Total
	Death of a Celebrity	Sept 2009	£6.99	
	A Highland Christmas	Nov 2009 (hardback)	£9.99	
	Death of a Village	Nov 2009	£6.99	
	Death of a Poison Pen	Nov 2009	£6.99	
	Death of a Valentine	Jan 2010 (hardback)	£18.99	
	Death of a Bore	Feb 2010	£6.99	
	Death of a Witch	Feb 2010	£6.99	
	Death of a Dreamer	Apr 2010	£6.99	
	Death of a Maid	Apr 2010	£6.99	
	Grand Total			£

FREEPOST RLUL-SJGC-SGKJ, Cash Sales Direct Mail Dept., The Book Service, Colchester Road, Frating, Colchester, CO7 7DW. Tel: +44 (0) 1206 255 800.
Fax: +44 (0) 1206 255 930. Email: sales@tbs-ltd.co.uk

UK customers: please allow £1.00 p&p for the first book, plus 50p for the second, and an additional 30p for each book thereafter, up to a maximum charge of £3.00. Overseas customers (incl. Ireland): please allow £2.00 p&p for the first book, plus £1.00 for the second, plus 50p for each additional book.

NAME (block letters): _____

ADDRESS: _____

_____

_____ POSTCODE: _____

I enclose a cheque/PO (payable to 'TBS Direct') for the amount

of £_____.

I wish to pay by Switch/Credit Card

Card number: _____

Expiry date: _____ Switch issue number: _____